Men of Mayhem and Vengeance

Lauren Biel

Copyright © 2022 by Lauren Biel

All rights reserved.

No part of this book may be reproduced in any form or by any electronic or mechanical means, including information storage and retrieval systems, without written permission from the author, except for the use of brief quotations in a book review.

This is a work of fiction. Names, characters, events, and incidents are the products of the author's imagination. Any resemblance to actual persons, living or dead, or actual events is purely coincidental.

Library of Congress Cataloging-in-Publication Data

Men of Mayhem & Vengeance/Lauren Biel 1st ed.

Printed in the United States of America

Cover Design: Laura Hidalgo of Spellbinding Design

Content Editing: Sugar Free Editing

Interior Design: Sugar Free Editing

For more information on this book and the author, visit: www.LaurenBiel.com

Please visit LaurenBiel.com for a full list of content warnings.

Men of Mayhem

Chapter 1

May 14th, 1931

Mama was breezing through the kitchen as I came out in my uniform. She looked worn down, her usually coiffed hair a mess of dark waves graying from stress. She was always in a rush. After my pops died in a machine accident a few years back, she remarried, took on her new husband's business, and became the seamstress at his tailoring company.

I chuckled to myself at the thought of my mama finding a husband, with her barren old womb, while every man I met skedaddled when they found out I couldn't have any children of my own. After a while, I started telling 'em right from the start. I'd grown sick of wasting my time and developing feelings, only to watch the deal break as they learned my secret later on. Every time I told them, they'd look at me with pity. Such a shame.

It was my fault. I'd gotten pregnant twice in my early twenties. Little did I know back then, when the doctor got rid of them, it meant I'd never have any more of my own. I wasn't sure if I'd have kept the pregnancies, even if I knew what I knew now. The second time, it was from the piece of shit who raped me in the alleyway behind the general store. I wasn't gonna carry his child. I didn't need the reminder of that night, every day, for the rest of my life.

"You could do a bit more with your hair, Silvia," my mother said as she walked over and drew my hair from the clip, letting my auburn waves fall to my shoulders.

I pawed her hands away. She had no idea what it was like to work in a hot and sweaty diner full of men and teenagers. She married my pops young and became a housewife like you're supposed to.

I grabbed my clip and wrapped my hair back up in it. I looked at the door, ready to walk down to the diner and start yet another shift from hell.

"Lookin' like that, it's no wonder you can't find yourself a husband," she called after me with a sneer.

No, I couldn't find a husband because no man wanted a fucking barren woman. They wanted someone who could keep their lineage going, and that person could never be me.

That was why I spent my days working in a diner I hated, only to come home to reminders of how much less of a woman I was.

I could never be anything more.

TRASH LITTERED THE DINER. I wiped down a table after a bunch of kids came in and made a mess of it. Would any of them leave their mama's kitchen looking like that? I scoffed as I brushed it all into the trash.

The bell rang above the door.

Fucking kids. "You better not have—" I started to say. When I turned around, it wasn't the kids running back in here again. It was two men. Big men.

I smoothed the skirt of my uniform and brushed a piece of loose auburn hair from my face. No one came in here looking like they did—suits and nice hats—and it made me feel that much sorer about myself and that rat-infested diner.

"Can I help you, fellas?" I asked as I left the table streaked with cleaner.

The tallest one, with short dark hair and darker eyes, just smiled at me. Not a friendly smile, but it wasn't entirely menacing, either. My heartbeat quickened in my chest. I wasn't too sure about him.

The other man took a step toward me, causing me to take an instinctive step back.

"We're closing up in a few minutes," I told them as I tossed the rag onto the bar counter.

"We'll wait," the grumpy looking one said, brushing a hand through nearly black hair. His eyes were almost as dark as the strands on his head.

Wait for what? Me? "Come again?"

"You're coming for a little ride," he explained. "It ain't nothing to worry about."

Sure didn't seem like nothing.

His voice was dark and deep, and his confidence almost made me take a step forward. When he leaned back, the pistol showed at his side, stopping the twitch of my muscles that almost moved me toward him. I swallowed hard.

"It's about your mama," he explained in a sterner tone.

Realization slapped me in the face. They were the men my mama and her new husband had to pay every month. I knew they hadn't paid in a little while, but I didn't expect them to come for *me*. It wasn't my damn business needing protection. Nothing in their expressions or statures made me think I was getting out of it. They had guns. I had a goddamn mop, and as good as I was with it, it wouldn't do jack to men like them.

"Are you going to kill me?" I asked as I untied my apron.

The question was much flatter than I intended. It should have been laced with fear, but I had little. I asked as if I needed to know what to expect.

"We ain't going to hurt you unless we have to," the man said, drawing a tight smile that made me more uncomfortable than when he just stood there frowning.

I followed them into the crisp spring air, and they guided me to their car. The weird, tall man held my shoulders while the other placed my hands behind my back and tied a raggedy rope around my wrists.

I narrowed my eyes at him. "Is this necessary?"

"Maybe not. We'll see," he said from behind me, his warm breath caressing the back of my neck.

They pushed me into the backseat of the car and took off, heading away from the city. I looked back, wondering what the hell was in store for me and why I had jack shit to do with any of it.

I should have been more afraid than I was. Yeah, there was fear, but also a brewing sense of . . . excitement? Curiosity? A desire to get the hell away from the diner? I felt like a dog just let off its leash, getting to see the big world for the first time as we drove away from the city I'd never stepped foot out of.

The fibers of the cheap rope rubbed my wrists raw, making my skin feel hot and itchy, and a pang in my bladder reminded me I hadn't gone to the bathroom since the afternoon lunch rush. Well, fuck. Hopefully it wouldn't be a long trip and I wouldn't end up chained to a post in some cellar.

No one spoke. The only thing that broke the silence was the occasional crackle of the cigar every time the driver inhaled. I liked the way it smelled—like a woodsy, sweet cigarette. He lifted his hand and brushed it through his dark hair.

I looked down at the rifle between them. It was an

ominous piece of metal that made me sweat. A pistol rested beneath the arm of the driver's pinstripe dress shirt. Every so often, his eyes met mine, and I dropped them away from him. He was quiet, but his presence hovered over everyone in the car. The man in the passenger seat was larger, but it was clear who called the shots.

The passenger laid his arm across the back of the seat and turned to face me. "What do we call you?" he asked.

I shrugged.

His eyes narrowed on me. "Suit yourself," he said before lighting up a cigarette.

I stared at it in longing. My mama didn't care if I was thirty, she'd still smack a cigarette out of my hand. I hadn't felt the effects of nicotine in nearly a decade. I worked in a diner, and everyone smoked while waiting for their meals. I couldn't get away from the damn things, but I also couldn't afford such a pricey habit. My eyes remained locked on the smoke billowing from the man's full lips.

"You want one?" he asked, holding the smoking cigarette between fingers on the biggest hand I'd ever seen. Sensing my desperation when I nodded too fast, he tugged it away. "Tell me your name."

"Silvia," I told him, not because I wanted to, but because I wanted that cigarette.

"Well, *Silvia*, I ain't spoon feeding you, so you'll have to wait."

"Cut her loose and give her a fuckin' smoke," the driver said.

The larger man's smile dropped from his face. "You think that's a good idea?"

"She came with us without a fight, Vernon. I doubt she'll go kickin' one up now."

I cocked my head as the passenger drew a knife. The metal blade glinted against the sun.

"Lean your ass over this way," he commanded.

I shuffled my body, scooting my back toward him. His hand reached out and gripped the rope, and he sawed at it until the fibers spread, giving me more leverage until the rope broke apart and settled beside me on the seat.

They were right about me not putting up a fight. I wouldn't fight men who were bigger than my own pops. No way. Vernon looked like he could snap me in two just by picking me up, and the other one just looked mean as hell. I didn't even have the choice to fight or flee. I was stuck in place, staring at these two men in their suits and fedoras since they said I had to come with them. What would they do if I said no? Nothing good, that's for sure.

I rubbed my wrists before reaching out and taking the cigarette from Vernon's outstretched arm. With a deep inhale, I sucked the smoke into my lungs and let it simmer for a while before blowing it back out. Smoke filled the car and swirled around us in a murky haze.

I coughed, forgetting how strong the nicotine would be. My body lurched with every spasm of my throat, and I half thought I'd piss myself. I looked down at the pale white stockings beneath my uniform as my bladder twitched. I *was* gonna piss myself.

"C-can we . . . stop," I choked out between coughs.

"What's the matter?" the driver asked.

"I have to pee." I stopped coughing and wiped the tears from my eyes.

"There's nothin' for miles."

"I could piss too," Vernon told the driver.

The man let out a gruff sound as he pulled onto the side of the road. I climbed out of the car. I didn't even think about running. My focus was on not soaking my stockings. I leaned against the door and tugged them down, pulling the thin fabric forward as I squatted.

Relief was immediate.

I tried to stop my stream as Vernon stepped from the car, undid his slacks, and pulled his dick out beside me. I kept my eyes locked ahead, ignoring the flushing red of my cheeks. Even though I wasn't trying to look at his dick, I couldn't stop it from creeping into my line of vision. The guy just stood there, staring at me, his dick hard as he pissed. I turned away.

"Keep your eyes on it, Silvia," he said with a laugh.

"No thanks."

I finished and tried to pull up my stockings. The warm humidity in the car left my skin sweaty, and the fabric caught on my thighs. Vernon shook off and stepped into me. His dick was still out, glaring at me as he took the knife from his waistband and reached between my legs. He tugged the fabric forward and cut it. He could have done it with his hands, but he sliced through my stockings, regardless.

I shivered at his rough touch.

"This seems unnecessary," I said. I leaned away from him as he sawed at the flimsy material.

"These are unnecessary," he said with a smirk as he pulled my stockings away from my pale legs and pocketed them. "Your outfit makes you look like a girl I knew, and she never wore these." He gestured to his pocket.

"Was she your girl?"

"She was."

"What happened to her?" I asked. I probably didn't want to know the answer.

Vernon tapped me on the nose with his knife. "The less questions you ask, the better." He zipped up his slacks.

As I reached for the door handle, I looked back at the road. I wanted to run, but part of me found this unknown better than the nothingness I'd run back to.

Mama said I'd never get married because I was barren. She was right. Men wanted a wife who could one day be a mother.

I could only be a wife, and even then, I'd probably be no good at it. I wasn't the quiet and meek woman I'd need to be. I was also never content and probably never would be, no matter what man I tried to marry.

"Better not think about running," Vernon said. His dark eyes somehow grew darker. "You're a bit too pretty to meet a bullet."

"Where would I even go?" I snapped.

"Back home to some husband?" the driver asked as I opened the door and sat in the backseat behind Vernon.

I shook my head. "Ain't got one."

"Told ya, Reaper. You owe me ten," Vernon said through a laugh.

Reaper? What a name. "You bet on if I was married?"

"Sure did. And you don't walk like no married woman." Vernon turned back toward me. "When was the last time you were laid on your back?"

"Vernon," Reaper said with a stern tone that made a dark smile cross Vernon's face. "That's not what she's here for."

"Yeah, yeah."

"She's just a quick incentive for her mama. She'll be with us for a few days, then she'll go on her merry way."

"But, boss . . ." Vernon groaned.

"No one touches a hair on her head."

"Her head ain't what I want to touch," Vernon said with a smirk.

Heat crept down my neck and mottled my chest. I was too embarrassed to even admit the last time I was with a man. Who the fuck knew?

I listened to them talk as I tugged off my shoes, pulled away what was left of my ripped stockings, and tossed the soft, dingy fabric scraps out the window. They played in the breeze before landing on the dust-covered road.

"I swear to God, Vernon, if you fuck this up, I'll kill you.

It's a simple fuckin' task. We hold her, get paid, and give her back so she can go back to her lonely life."

"It's not lonely," I told them, but the crack in my voice betrayed the lie I tried to tell. It *was* a lonely life. I would probably die alone, and I couldn't even chase away my feelings with a goddamn drink. We were in the midst of prohibition with no end in sight.

Chapter 2

Reaper and Vernon led me to the front door of a small home in the middle of nowhere. Overgrown grass stretched in every direction for as far as I could see.

"You guys live here?" I asked as I walked up the ramshackle steps. The door's glass pane had been shattered, and our feet crunched on the fallen shards as we stepped closer. "Guess not."

"Smart mouth on you," Reaper said as he pushed past me. "No wonder you ain't got a husband."

Vernon stared at me like a cat with a cornered mouse. He gestured inside and followed after me.

Glass shattered.

I snapped my attention toward the noise, and my eyes landed on a shaggy blond-haired man who had dropped his glass at the sight of me. His blue eyes were on me, roving over my body.

"Who . . . is this?" he asked.

"Don't get your hopes up, Ricky. She's just a *quick incentive*," Vernon said with a smirk.

I felt unconvinced that was all I was. My mama didn't

have the money to pay. If she had, I wouldn't have been there at all. Part of me knew I'd never leave. They'd probably kill me, and there'd be nothing to mourn of the lonely life I'd lose. But I'd meet my end at the hands of three of the best-looking men I'd seen in a long while. Worse ways to go out, I guess.

Reaper brought in a glass of clear liquid and handed it to me. I tried to down it, thinking it was water. The second the moonshine hit the back of my throat, I regretted the huge swig. It burned as it moved along my esophagus and buried itself in my stomach. I squeezed my eyes closed and fought the urge to vomit.

"Fuck, that's horrible," I said as I wiped my mouth.

Vernon chuckled. "What haven't you had longer? A drink or a man?"

I glared at him. I couldn't remember which I had last. Pathetic. "Fuck you," I snarled. I wasn't going to leave this house alive, but I also wasn't going to kiss their asses for my last few days on earth.

Reaper laughed, which made Vernon tighten his lips.

"One hair?" Vernon asked.

Reaper sobered up, realizing what he was asking. "Don't ask that again. And get her stockings out of your goddamn pocket."

Vernon growled as he took the balled-up fabric from his pocket and put it up to his nose. "It smells like her pussy."

I dropped my jaw, and my cheeks flamed hot. He was disgusting.

Ricky, who had busied himself by picking up the glass shards, shot his gaze toward Vernon. "That's no way to talk about a lady, Vernon."

"What are you gonna do about it?" Vernon shot back. When Ricky's lips formed a thin line, Vernon nodded. "Exactly."

Ricky tightened his fist until the glass sank into his palm. A thick line of blood rolled through his clenched fingers.

Vernon took a step into me and inhaled. "I can't touch you, but these will do," he said as he wadded the stockings in his hand.

I TOSSED and turned in bed because it wasn't familiar. It smelled like dust and mold inside the dark room, and the air suffocated me with a damp heaviness. I didn't know how anybody slept in here.

I crawled out of bed and went into the living room, my feet sticking on the old wood floor. The boys were still awake. Glasses surrounded them, some of which were upside down or on their sides. Everyone seemed light and happy. Their eyes shot to me when I came into the room.

Reaper smirked before nodding at me. "If you're going to stand there, you might as well come have a drink."

Vernon sneered. "She couldn't even handle the first drink."

I couldn't *not* handle the drink. It was just unexpected. I hadn't prepared my throat for a liquid as noxious as backyard moonshine. It had been so dry around the city that I didn't expect it to be any type of alcohol, so fuck him. I used to be able to drink a man like him under the table.

I strolled over to Vernon and grabbed the glass that he was drinking from. Without hesitation, I downed the potent liquor. His eyes lit up, and blood rushed to his dick.

"Well, that's not fair. You broads can just open your throats and take whatever we spill down them." Vernon waved me off.

"You got any more? I'll show you how much I can open my throat."

Ricky stopped spinning the knife between his fingers and raised his eyebrow at me. I said what I said.

"Are you trying to challenge me to a drinking game?" Vernon smirked. The flush of his cheeks showed he was already half soused.

"That's a bad fucking idea, Vernon," Reaper warned.

"I think it's a great one," Vernon said as he tossed me an old Mason jar they were using as a glass. He grabbed a larger jar which was filled with the toxic, clear liquor. Even from a few feet away, the sharp scent of alcohol singed my sinuses.

Vernon sat on the floor and crossed his legs in a way I didn't expect such a big man to be able to do. The jar of liquor slammed down in front of him. I sat down, drawing my legs beneath me, and grazed my finger along the grooved rim of the jar in my lap. Ricky hopped down between us and poured liquor into our glasses. He looked at me, his features soft and playful. He was nothing like the other two, but he was so goddamn handsome all the same.

"Drink," he called out.

I lifted my glass and threw it back, taking as much of the lip-curling liquor as I could in one swig. I threw my glass to the floor just as Vernon dropped his. Ricky filled them right back up. I tossed my head back and swallowed a whole mouthful, emptying my glass a mere second before Vernon, my throat numb to the liquor's assault. Ricky filled them one last time. Vernon lifted his glass but kept his eyes on me as I downed my last drink. He watched my throat as I swallowed. The alcohol crawled through me and warmed my body, painting my cheeks a warm pink. When I dropped my glass to the floor, they were all staring at me.

"Get those eyes off her, Vernon," Reaper commanded.

"Just a taste." He growled as he sat up on his knees.

He looked like a predator, poised to strike. I was prey. They'd mistaken my quietness for weakness, when it made me the strongest of them all. I didn't show fear as a drunk and crazed Vernon reached out for me, fisted my hair, and tugged me toward his mouth. The scent of moonshine hung in the air between us.

The *click* of a cocked gun made Ricky tense. I looked up at Reaper, who had aimed his pistol at Vernon.

"I said, no."

Vernon narrowed his eyes at me, and a pang of excitement shuddered through me as his hand released my hair. I sat back on my heels. If Reaper hadn't called it off and reined in the beast, he would have pounced and taken his kill. That shouldn't have been as pleasant of a thought as it was.

The room was electrified. I let my eyes rise up Reaper's body beside me. He met my gaze.

"Don't fuckin' look at me like that, doll. I'm only keeping you from him because he'll tear you to shreds." He gestured toward Vernon, whose dick still painfully pressed against the front of his pants.

"I would," Vernon said with a quick rise in his chest.

Why was I okay with that? I shouldn't have been. These men preyed on people like my mama and their businesses. They thrived because of the fear they instilled, but for some reason, I wasn't afraid of them.

Chapter 3

Vernon and Reaper went to talk to my mama. They wanted to intimidate her and make sure she knew who took her daughter. It pained me to know how broken hearted she'd be. If she couldn't pay—and I knew she couldn't—she'd carry so much guilt for the rest of her days. The worst part? I was being held for ransom for a business that wasn't even hers to begin with. She married into it. His debt became hers.

It never failed to make me chuckle when I thought about my mama finding another husband so easily. The laugh was rooted in jealousy, at a woman like her finding not one but two husbands, even when she could no longer give him any other children. He liked her for her, and that blew my mind.

"Why you laughing?" Ricky asked.

He was clearly my babysitter—someone to watch me and make sure I didn't run.

Where would I go?

"Nothing. Just life." I shrugged.

Ricky raised his eyebrows at me.

"Got any kids?" I asked. He looked like a father. The others looked like gangsters, but Ricky? He had the most angelic face I'd ever seen. While he was strong, he was that thin type of muscular that made him stick out between the other two. He looked like he could be a husband.

"Nah, never had much of an interest in little ones running around. You?"

I frowned and dropped my gaze. Shaking my head, I met his eyes again. "Can't."

"It's okay. Who needs 'em? I was almost an uncle, though. My brother knocked up his old lady about three months before he died. She was so broken up about it that she lost the baby."

"What happened to your brother?"

"That's a story for another day." He turned away from me. "Did you sleep okay last night?"

What an odd question. "Nah, there's nothing comfortable about sleeping in a strange bed with strange men around. I hardly slept at all." Which was true. I tossed and turned on the uncomfortable mattress, alternating between being too exhausted to get up and make a run for it and too worked up to sleep. I must have fallen asleep at some point because I woke up to the house blanketed in darkness and only the bones of the old building creaking with sound.

"We aren't all strange," he said with a smile. "Is there something I can do to make it more comfortable for you?"

His question took me off guard. Why would he care about making me comfortable when I was a quick hold? Whether my mama paid or they killed me off, I wouldn't be here for very long. I should be glad I had a bed at all.

His smile was sweet and generous, as if he meant every word. As if he'd lay out a cloud if he could, just to make me more comfortable. Ricky seemed so out of place here. He had a youthful expression that seemed so innocent. Like an angel among the demons. Angel. That's what I was gonna call him.

The door swung open and Vernon came in, dragging a

writhing man behind him by his suit. He shot me a sadistic smile as he continued toward the back of the house. The man's screams echoed as the sound receded. Reaper came in behind him, blood on his white shirt.

"I thought you were going to talk to my mama?"

"We did. She ain't willing to pay, which makes me wonder how much you're really worth. I'm giving her until Sunday."

"Then where'd he come from?" I gestured toward the back room where the man began to scream as if he were dying.

He probably was.

"Oh, that? Nothin' to worry your pretty head about. Sometimes you just cross paths by chance with someone who wronged you. Ricky, can you make sure Vernon doesn't leave any fuckin' body parts laying around this time?" Reaper commanded.

Ricky sneered but got up and followed the weakening screams.

"Vernon thinks it's funny to leave pieces of people on our goddamn pillows," Reaper continued. "Like a cat bringing you a mouse he half chewed." He smiled as he sat beside me. He smelled like blood and sweat.

Reaper was built as if he'd grown up doing manual labor all his life. He was massive and strong, but he wasn't all muscle like Vernon. His chest was broad and his shoulders wide. He was built to work.

"I'm guessing Reaper isn't your God given name?"

"Of course not. There ain't no God around here, doll. But if I told you my real name, I'd have to kill you." His expression was so flat that I couldn't tell if he was kidding. I'd have wagered that he probably was not.

"Why do they call you Reaper?" I asked, though I had a pretty good idea.

He reached back with a smile and drew his pistol. My mouth dropped open as he laid it out on his large palm and showcased it. There were lines etched into the metal. "I ran outta space," he said with a rise in his chest, as if proud of himself.

"Are . . . are those . . . people you've killed?" I sputtered.

Reaper let a smile cross his face, but he didn't respond. He looked as if he expected his admittance to bother me, but he was also brooding with pride, and it made my lips turn upward.

I wasn't surprised he was a killer. He was the goddamn Reaper, after all.

"You ain't like most broads, you know?" Reaper's expression sobered, and his gaze left mine. The rigidity of his posture made me uncomfortable as it shifted the air in the room.

"What's gonna happen to me if my mama doesn't pay?" I got up the courage to finally ask after tense minutes of silence.

"We'll cross that bridge when we get to it," he said dismissively as he stood up and left me on the couch.

My head swam and the fear finally ripped through me—the emotion that should have been coursing through me since the beginning. Even then, I still didn't make a move to leave. To run.

They'd find me. I'd meet the Reaper whether I was here or home.

The front door opened, startling me from my panic, and a man I hadn't seen before entered the house. We both shared the same expression of surprise. He wasn't big and strong like Reaper and Vernon, not as angelic as Ricky, but he was something right in the middle. Intimidating in a way I could hardly describe. Darkness lurked behind his arrogant smirk. Our eyes met, and the intensity of his icy gaze made me swallow hard.

Reaper walked into the room, demanding our attention

with a deep clearing of his throat. "I didn't think you were coming till tomorrow," Reaper said to the man.

"Took an earlier train. Who is she?" He looked back at me.

"The incentive," Reaper said with tight lips.

"A goddamn good one." The man walked over to me and offered his hand. "There's not a human on earth who knows my name, but you can call me Morris." He removed his hat and clutched it to his chest.

My eyes climbed up his crisp suit and landed on his dark hair and haunting gray eyes. "Silvia," I replied, still mesmerized.

"Nice to meet you, sweets." His words were smooth, as if he were a businessman instead of a mobster.

"We got business to discuss, Morris. Lift your jaw off the floor and come on," Reaper said as his steps receded.

"Pleasure to meet you. I hope they've been treating you well," Morris said before following Reaper.

They had . . . so far.

Chapter 4

Me and the men had opposite sleep schedules, which meant I didn't really get much sleep there. I walked out of the bedroom, chasing the sounds of laughter and wearing only my slip, which stopped at my thighs.

All four men sobered up as I walked into the room. They'd dragged the dining room table to the middle of the floor. They sat around it, playing cards, drinking, and smoking.

Vernon pulled out a cigarette when I squeezed past the table. "You want one?" he asked.

I nodded.

"Beg for it."

"I don't want it that bad," I said. I wasn't begging for what I wasn't even supposed to be doing in the first place. Also, fuck him.

"Here, sweets," Morris said as he handed me what was left of his.

I took it, flashing a smug gaze back at Vernon.

"Who put the bloody finger in the pot of money,

Vernon?" Reaper asked with a glare. Even after only two days with them, I knew it was that crazy son of a bitch.

Vernon smirked. "It's not the finger. It's what's *on* the finger."

Reaper picked it up and examined it. A ring encased the swelling flesh. "You ain't right," he said as he threw the finger aside.

"You don't like what I put in to play with? I got something else." Vernon glanced my way. "What about whoever wins the next hand gets her?"

Gets her? Me? Nah. We weren't playing a game where I was the pot to win.

"She isn't something to bet on, Vernon," Ricky said as he shuffled the deck. "Don't be such a dick."

I sat down at the dilapidated table and leaned forward, my elbows dropping to my pale thighs. "How can you throw my pussy in the pot when you haven't even asked if I'd like to play?"

Morris choked on his drink, swallowing hard before coughing. Ricky smirked behind the hand curled over his chin.

Reaper laughed. "Broads don't get to play with the men. Not this way, at least."

"How about this? If I win this next hand, no one *gets me*. If I lose, I'll sleep with one of you."

Reaper narrowed his eyes at me. "You're out of your mind, doll."

"Maybe." I was having fun. It was excitement I hadn't had in . . . well, in my entire life.

Ricky dealt the cards. Queen, five—a real dicey fucking hand to be dealt. I looked around at the men before lowering my cards. The tension was so thick that I could feel it squeezing me. I swallowed.

"How would we even choose who you're going to fuck?" Vernon asked.

"Lady's choice," Morris responded.

Vernon scoffed. "Well that's shit. She ain't gonna choose—"

"You? Nah, probably not," Reaper said with a laugh as he squelched his cigar out in the tray. A wisp of blue-gray smoke curled toward my nose. "Don't get wrapped up in it, Vernon. She wouldn't choose me, either. She'd choose one of the nice ones over there." He gestured to Ricky and Morris. "She has to know neither of us would be a wise choice."

I glared at him. His words made me flush with nerves, and as Ricky laid out the flop, it only worsened. He flipped the first three cards in the center, and I hit a pair of fives. That sure as shit wasn't gonna help me get out of the bet I made.

"Cheeks are real red, doll," Reaper said. "You thinking about which of those two you wanna take into your bed tonight?"

"Fuck you," I said beneath my breath. But not low enough.

Reaper's lips tightened as if no woman had ever talked to him like that. They probably hadn't. Or at least didn't live to tell about it if they had.

Ricky added a fourth card to the center of the table. Another five. Three of a kind? Not the worst hand, but was it good enough? I looked at Vernon's eyes. They were crazed, as if he had something better.

"I say, winner gets her," Vernon quipped.

"That confident in your hand?" Morris asked.

"Wishful fucking thinking." Vernon licked his lips. His leg shook beneath the table, tapping his foot against the floor.

Ricky reached over and flipped the last card. A fucking queen. Full house. Fuck yes! I turned my cards over and threw them onto the table.

Morris and Ricky tossed their hands down with a groan. Reaper turned over his cards, showcasing a flush. An admirable hand. Vernon curled his lip as he threw down a straight—one he'd clearly pinned high hopes on.

"Well, shit. Beginner's luck, eh?" Reaper said with a pinched, disappointed smile.

Vernon sat there, seething. His cheeks pulsed with anger.

Reaper slid his chair back, stood, and leaned over me. "Don't worry, doll. We were just havin' fun. I wouldn't have let any of us fuck you." He set his jaw and backed away from me. "Who needs another drink?"

Just as Ricky reached out his hand and started gathering the cards, I realized I'd hoped I'd lose. I shouldn't have felt this much disappointment from a win.

It felt more like I'd lost.

As crazy as it sounded in my own head, the thought of getting beneath any of the four men excited me in a way I couldn't understand. Brief fantasies formed against my will. I wanted to feel small beneath Reaper's stocky frame as he took me. I wanted my angel to make love to me, soft and slow, while I looked into his blue eyes. Morris seemed like he could teach me a thing or two about my own body. And Vernon . . . I couldn't fathom what he would do to me, but for some sick reason, I wanted to find out.

I HEARD them talking about me in the other room. I kept my back pinned to the bedroom wall as I listened.

What sounded like Reaper's voice floated over to me. "They ain't paid."

"What are we gonna do with her?" Vernon's thick, deep voice asked.

I leaned harder into the wood behind me, hoping to hear Reaper's response. I heard nothing. He either whispered it or gestured something... or ignored the question completely.

I walked toward the living room, sneaking past a new conversation between the men. White-hot rage filled me until I saw red. I'd finally found an interesting life with interesting people, yet they only saw me as a pawn in their game. I was more than that, and I wouldn't go out quietly. Maybe they were used to simpering females, but that wasn't me.

My eyes fell upon a fire poker. I snatched it up, stormed into the kitchen, and raised the cold metal to my shoulder.

Reaper stared at me, unfazed by my threat. "What are you doin', doll? Put that down before you hurt yourself."

"Fuck you! If you're going to kill me, at least have the balls to tell me to my face!"

Vernon kept a lustful expression. "Better watch yourself. I wouldn't be wielding something you got no business swinging. What are you gonna do?"

I swung at Vernon as he approached, but he caught it and jerked my arm back, bending my wrist until I dropped the poker. It thudded against the floor. His body pressed behind me, still twisting my arm. The weight of his hard cock pressed against my lower back.

"Fuck you!" I writhed against him, but it was futile. He was too damn strong.

I cried, not from sadness, but from frustration. He released my arm, and I fell into him. He kept his hands at his sides.

"Yeah, I don't do crying," he said as he righted me so he could get out from behind me. "Rather you hit me with the damn poker than ask me to comfort you."

"You guys are such assholes!" I shrieked. It was all out of

anger. I was sick of the unknown. If tomorrow was my last day on this godforsaken earth, I wanted to know about it!

"Your mama still has a day to pay, and we haven't figured out what we're doing with you yet. You need to relax." Reaper's voice was stern, and it was clear why he was the leader in the way he spoke—so confident and even, as if nothing could razzle him. He pointed at the poker. "You're lucky I didn't put a bullet through that pretty head of yours for that shit. You don't threaten me or my men, do you understand?" He grabbed my chin.

"Then don't threaten me." I ripped my chin away from his touch and stormed out of the room.

His laughter mocked me from behind.

Maybe I should have run, after all.

Chapter 5

When I walked into the living room, the weight of something ominous pressed in on me from all sides. Ricky and Morris looked somber. My mama hadn't paid. She couldn't. I stared at the sunlight shining through the tattered curtains.

I hadn't slept a wink last night. I was too worried about what would happen to me. I wasn't all that afraid, but the guessing drove me loony. I always knew what they would do to me once they didn't get their money, but I never expected them to leave me untouched. I expected them to force me. To use me. I knew they wanted me because I saw it in the ebb and flow of their hard dicks every time I was around. No one made a move without Reaper's permission, though, and it was clear he wouldn't give it.

In a way, I was a bit disappointed. It had been so long since I'd been with a man. It would have been nice to experience one of them before meeting my end. I cursed myself for winning at poker. It was my chance, and I lost it by winning.

Vernon grabbed me from behind. I flailed, swinging my legs to try to hit him in the goddamn nuts. He wrapped a powerful arm around my waist and pinned me against him. Reaper dragged a chair into the middle of the room, and Vernon set me on it like a child.

"Get it over with," Morris said to Reaper. Unable to watch what was about to happen to me, his steps receded.

Vernon looked at me with equal parts desire and hatred in his crazed eyes. Reaper stepped in front of me with heavy footfalls and drew his pistol from its holster. His jaw clenched, making his cheeks pulse. He wiped a hand through hair so dark you could mistake it for the hood of Grim's robe.

"You know we can't keep you," he said with a slow draw of his words as he cocked the revolver. "And we sure as shit can't let you go."

I stared down the barrel of his Colt, unwilling to plead for my life. They were going to do what they were going to do whether I begged or not. Reaper took another step toward me and touched the barrel to my forehead. His finger trembled as he went to curl it around the trigger. I closed my eyes, awaiting the millisecond of explosive sound before I'd feel nothing at all.

There was a small sense of betrayal, even though I'd known what was coming. It didn't matter that we shared drinks or played games together. It didn't matter that I never tried to run from them. They couldn't keep me around. There was no room for a girl like me in their group. I was a lonely woman with nothing to go home to, and they were lawless men.

I didn't know if it was the desperation of the situation or the lack of intimacy in my life, but I'd started to feel a bit for them. They were all so different. Reaper had a no-nonsense demeanor that made me feel equally scared and safe. The mysteriousness of Morris intrigued me. I had even started to enjoy the pushy nature of Vernon. But I'd grown especially fond of Ricky, the sweet one who seemed like he didn't belong, much like me.

My thoughts drifted to my mama and the business, and I let a single tear fall down my cheek. It wasn't over for her, even if I was long gone. My death only left her with nothing else to bargain with.

"Goddamn it," Reaper whispered beneath the sound of the uncocked hammer. "I'm gonna regret the fuck out of this."

Ricky's eyes shot to us from across the room. Reaper lowered the pistol, his cheeks flushed with anger. The emotion wasn't directed at me, but at himself. What needed to be done was for the good of the business—their lifestyle—but even considering all of that, he couldn't do it.

The Reaper threatened but spared me, showing mercy I never expected.

I defied death itself.

Reaper fisted my auburn hair, a deep shade of red so dark it was almost brown. He drew my mouth to his. "Don't make me fuckin' regret this." His lips remained close to mine as he slipped his pistol back into the holster. "You're free to go, Silvia."

"What?" Vernon shouted. "What do you mean, she's free to go? No, that's not what we—"

Reaper snapped his glare to Vernon, who was seething with anger over who the fuck knew what. "What I say, goes. It doesn't matter what I said yesterday. You, doll, are free to leave."

"But she's seen our faces. Knows some of our names." Morris gestured toward Vernon and Ricky.

"I don't want to go," I whispered beneath their arguing.

"She could turn us in the moment she walks the hell outta here!" Vernon yelled, his voice so deep and angry it made me shiver.

"Who the hell cares if she does? Most of us are already wanted, anyway," Reaper said with a sneer.

"I said, I don't want to go!" I yelled over them.

They turned toward me.

"Come again?" Reaper asked.

"I want to stay here," I said, dropping my gaze to the floor.

Reaper narrowed his eyes as if he was trying to figure out what the fuck to do with me. Vernon went dead silent. He liked the idea; I was sure of it. Ricky had a sweet, hopeful look on his face, and I couldn't tell if he wanted me to stay or get the hell out of there while I still could.

"We can't keep you, doll. You just—it's just not a good idea."

"Bad for business," Morris agreed.

"If you all don't want her, I'd happily keep her," Vernon said with a smirk. The dangerous twitch of his lips warmed my skin.

"We all know what you do to your molls." Morris shook his head. "Better off forcing her to get instead of giving her to him."

Reaper stayed quiet. Brooding. Trying to figure out what he wanted to do. He grabbed me around the waist and carried me to the bedroom. He set me on the bed and stared at me with dark, intense eyes. "Convince me," he said

"To what?" My eyes dropped to the tented slacks in front of my face.

"To keep you," he said in a tone that made me melt into the firm mattress.

Half of me was angered by his statement. I didn't need to prove myself to him. The other half of me—the dominant half—said "fuck you" to my dignity.

He reached toward me and tugged at the straps of my slip. The fabric fell down my chest and exposed the pale skin of my breasts. He growled when the thin fabric remained over my nipples.

"You better take that off before I rip it off you."

I swallowed hard. It was pretty much all I had besides my damn uniform. I got to my feet, lifted it over my head, and stood naked in front of him. Insecurity pulsed through me as his eyes scanned my body.

"I ain't gonna go easy on you," he said. His lips met mine, hard, fast, and with a passion I'd never felt. He growled as he kissed me. He pulled away and looked down at me. "Ricky told me you can't have kids. Is that true?"

He turned me around, pulled me into his hard body, and worked off his buckle behind me. I nodded and looked back at him. I expected him to get the same disappointed expression that most every man got who had an ache in his balls to have children, but a smile crawled across his face.

"I ain't ever wanted kids," Reaper said as he bent me over the bed. "I love the act of making 'em, though." His strong, rough hand grazed the bare skin of my back. "The thought of being able to fuck you without worrying about that? To only think about coming inside you? Fuck. That's almost reason enough to keep you."

I twitched between my legs. His words made me forget he planned to execute me only minutes earlier. I was willing to let the reaper fuck me for my life.

He pushed himself inside me, and I moaned as he sank deeper. He was big, and it'd been so damn long. The moment I was around him, he groaned.

"Fuck, doll. You feel incredible."

"Convinced yet?" I said with a strained voice as he wasted no time pulling out and thrusting back into me. His rough hands grabbed my ass as he pounded me harder than I'd ever experienced. More than I ever thought I could take. The pain coddled pleasure as his thrusts transformed what I felt.

I looked back to the doorway and saw Vernon. I made a move to pull away from Reaper, but he tugged me back in place.

He lifted my chest and ran a hand between my breasts. "Don't worry, he just likes to watch."

"I—"

"We're kind of a package deal, doll. He ain't ever going away. None of them are. Just focus on me and how I feel against your perfect fuckin' ass."

I relaxed into him, trying to ignore the fact that Vernon had leaned against the doorway and pulled out his dick. He rubbed himself in long strokes as he watched Reaper fuck me. Somehow, it turned me on even more.

My eyes locked on Vernon's as Reaper fucked me mercilessly from behind. His hand raced between the valley of my breasts, rising up to grip my throat in a possessive show of force.

The growl that came from Reaper at the sight of Vernon watching us made me shiver. It vibrated my body as his breath rolled over the sweaty curve of my neck. Vernon looked so intense, as if he'd fight Reaper to be the one behind me. If he did, it would be a massive display of brute strength. It would be primal. It would be fucking beautiful. They'd fight for me, and I almost craved it.

Vernon looked like he wanted to devour me. Hunger dripped from him as Reaper dripped his into me. I didn't fight my moans, letting them leave my lips freely as I dropped my head back and let Reaper's rhythmic strokes lull me. I focused on the hard pulse of his hips against my ass.

"I want to be deeper inside you, doll." Reaper released my chest, forcing me back onto my elbows. His large hand encased the back of my neck as he pushed his weight into me.

Pain mixed with my moans—a small scream woven within the sounds of pleasure. He was so deep. Too fucking deep. He didn't ask me if I was okay and didn't seem to care if I was, but I didn't expect him to be giving or gentle. The selfish way he fucked me was what I wanted from him.

Vernon bit his lip in a show of stifled frustration. My eyes roved down to the gentle heaving of his chest as he chased his pleasure, then continued further until they stopped at his dick. Vernon's strokes began to focus on his head. The muscles in his arms flexed as he tightened his grip on himself. He groaned and dropped his head back as he caught his come with his other hand. I cocked my head as he let go of his spent dick and brought his hand to his mouth, lapping up his come. There was something not right about him, yet I couldn't stop staring as his broad tongue licked up his palm. I imagined it on my pussy instead.

Reaper groaned behind me. "I'm going to fill you up, doll." When he lifted my chest, pressing my sweat covered back to his chest, he leaned his mouth close to my ear. "I'm so goddamn convinced," he said as he finished inside me.

Oh fuck, what was I doing? What had I gotten myself into?

Chapter 6

I wore Reaper's shirt, the fabric soft and warm against my skin. It was so big on me that the hem stopped at my thighs.

"You wanna play spades?" Ricky asked when I came into the room. He sat at a table with Vernon and Morris, shuffling a deck of cards.

I shrugged. "I haven't played before."

Vernon scoffed. "But you can play poker?"

Ricky continued shuffling the deck. "Spades trump all. I'll explain the rules as we go." He dealt thirteen cards to each of us. "Aces high, twos low," he said as he placed the deck beside him. "Now we bid."

I picked up the stack of cards and looked at the array of numbers. "On what?"

"How many tricks you think you can take," Vernon said with a smirk.

I narrowed my eyes at him, realizing he wasn't just talking about cards. "One?" I said.

"You're really low balling, love," Ricky said, oblivious to the tension between me and Vernon. "I bid three."

Vernon bid four and Morris bid five.

Ricky explained the rest of the game as we went, but it became hard to focus with Vernon fucking me with his eyes. After I made three tricks, I felt Vernon's hand on my thigh beneath the table. His fingers dug into me before climbing further. I grabbed his wrist and tried to stop him, but it was impossible. He was too damn strong and determined. His fingers pushed inside me as I tried to close my thighs.

Fuck.

I laid another card among the others, trying to keep my hands busy as I fanned the cards out in front of me. His thumb circled my clit when he drew his hand out, coating me in my wetness. I jolted. I met his dark and crazy eyes and found them hungrier than ever.

"Yeah, I can't wait for you." He growled and pushed the table aside. Cards slid across the wood. He leaned into me and before I knew what was happening, his mouth was a fraction of an inch from mine.

"Vernon!" Reaper called out as he walked into the room. "Don't overwhelm the girl. Get your damn hands off her."

"Goddamn it, boss, she looked like she felt incredible."

"Oh, she fuckin' did." Reaper's words made my cheeks flush.

Vernon raked his nails down my thigh as he pulled his hand away. His eyes locked on mine, and he licked up his fingers, a deep growl following the last motion of his tongue.

"Best pussy I've ever had. Without contest," Reaper said.

"Fuck." Vernon groaned. "You and I need to take this outside," he said, locking eyes with Reaper.

"I ain't fighting you right now, Vernon."

"If I don't take my frustration out somewhere, I'm gonna take it out on her."

Reaper stepped toward Vernon, and I backpedaled as Vernon's huge body went for him. Ricky crossed his leg over his lap when he sat down on the chair across the room. Morris threw a pocket knife up and caught it as he watched.

Reaper and Vernon clashed. I squealed as they pushed furniture aside with the force of their bodies. Reaper landed punches beneath Vernon's ribs, and Vernon met the pummeling with his own to Reaper's side. The sounds of fists on flesh echoed around me as they fought each other. There was little hesitation in their flexing muscles as the fight continued. They grappled, wrapped in a tight and forceful embrace, fists and arms flying out from every direction. There was no way to tell who was winning. They were both strong and so big. Too cut out for fighting.

"Guys!" I yelled over the madness. No one stopped. If anything, the sound of my voice made them fight harder.

"Don't bother, love," Ricky said. "They'll tire themselves out."

I sat back and kept my hand pressed over my mouth. I leaned my elbows onto my knees and kept my thighs clenched together, not just to avoid giving Ricky and Morris more of a glimpse, but because two men fighting over me made me twitch.

Inhuman grunts came from Vernon, and as he punched Reaper in the face with a quick jab, I swore I heard bones crunch. Reaper took a step back and clutched his nose. Blood spilled around his fingers in big crimson drops that slipped down his wrist.

"Cheap shot," Reaper snarled.

Vernon shook out his hand. "Don't be sour, boss. I fight for a living."

"What kind of fighting?" I asked as I removed my hand from my mouth.

"Street fights." Vernon walked into me and lifted my chin with a bloody hand. "And I always win."

I kept my eyes locked on his chest as it continued to rise and fall from his fight.

Reaper walked over and tugged me to my feet. He drew his hand away, revealing a bloody mouth and chin. It stained his shirt. He checked to see if the bleeding had stopped before he pulled me toward my bedroom and put me against the wall.

"What do you want?" he asked.

I cocked my head. "What do you mean?"

"Vernon. Do you want him?" Reaper wiped at his bloody chin with the back of his hand. "If you want it, I won't keep stopping him, doll. If you don't, I'll keep him off you."

I dropped my shoulders. "You don't want me?"

"Oh fuck, I want you." His dark eyes locked on mine "But he wants you too."

"I don't follow."

"You can have us both," Reaper said. "I just need to know what *you* want."

I was too struck by his words to respond. I never thought such things were possible. Both of them? How was I supposed to answer him? Vernon was terrifying, but he was so goddamn handsome. I was torn.

"I don't know..."

"Do you want me to stop him next time?"

I didn't say no, but I also didn't say yes. I just swallowed hard and finally shook my head.

"Be careful with him, doll. He ain't gonna go easy on you when he gets his hands on you."

I knew that. There was nothing kind or gentle about Vernon, but there was something that made me wonder, made me curious about what that kind of crazy would feel like inside me.

No inhibition.

Pure greed.

Hunger.

I wanted all of it, and Reaper gave his blessing. I could have both of them.

Reaper leaned into me and kissed me. The metallic taste of blood hit my tongue as he pushed inside my mouth. He groaned as he fisted my hair and rubbed his hand down my neck. His rough skin trailed down and stopped at the flushed skin of my chest.

"Why do I feel like you're going to cause a whole lot of trouble for us?" he said against my mouth. "Just don't make me regret taking you into my family."

Family? I'd never really had a family. Once my pops died and my mama remarried, I was alone. They had been right; I lived a very lonely life. The thought of being taken under their wings made my heart flutter. So many wings to stay safe beneath. But there were also so many beaks to tear at my flesh. I was torn between the safety and the danger.

While the thought of being fucked by two of these men excited me in ways I couldn't explain, I wasn't blind to the dangers of my situation. These were wanted men, and by sticking with them, I was committing myself to a life of crime. Me. A good girl who always did what her mama told her and kept her nose clean.

The thought of leaving made me cringe. It didn't even seem like an option. Not yet, at least. I was having *fun* for once in my life. And yeah, I liked them and all, but they were my shiny new toys as much as I was theirs. It wasn't much deeper than that. When things stopped being fun, I could just leave and go back to my old life.

My old, boring, lonely life.

"What about my mama?" I asked Reaper. No matter how often she made me feel bad about myself, she was still my mama. I wanted her to be safe.

His hand brushed the hair from my face, leaving a streak

of red-tinged sweat on my cheek. "Consider her debt repaid, doll."

"No more?"

"That's it."

"You'd do that?" I asked. I couldn't believe he'd wipe out her debt.

"Sinking into you is fuckin' priceless," Reaper growled.

I felt like the luckiest girl. I'd fixed things for my mama while finding a place that felt more like a home than the home I'd known. They were beginning to feel like the family I'd never had.

Chapter 7

Vernon pressed his hips against my ass as his hand rode along the rifle's slick metal. He covered my hand with his. The entire time he was trying to "teach" me, his hard dick rubbed against my ass, and I struggled to focus with his frustrated breath rolling over me.

"Why are you teaching me and not Reaper? I think a pistol would be easier to learn with, no?"

"A pistol takes skill. Precision. You can spray bullets with this bad boy. Even a woman should be able to kill something with this."

"Has anyone ever told you that you're real fucking rude?"

"Plenty," he responded with a shrug.

"What's Reaper's real name?" I asked as I put the rifle's butt against the pocket of my shoulder.

Vernon laughed. "Robert, but don't ever call him that. He'll kill you for it."

Vernon guided me as I curled my finger around the trigger, aiming the barrel at a tree trunk in front of us. Wood chipped off as I hit it, and a melodic noise reverberated beneath the deafening shot. The rhythmic, staccato sounds left my ears ringing.

"You're a goddamn natural," he said, and his words made me swell with pride.

He leaned into me and buried his nose in the crook of my neck. "That dress Reaper got you looks . . . fuck," he growled.

I glanced down at the dark purple dress. It was perfect. Better than anything I'd ever been able to afford.

"You know . . ." he began. The air around us grew thick and heavy as Vernon's posture stiffened. He pulled the rifle from my grasp. "I kept hoping you'd run so I'd have to catch you. Reaper said if you took off, I could do what I wanted to you before I killed you. But you didn't, did you?"

I shook my head.

"Run," he commanded.

"I'm not—"

The deafening sound of a gunshot at my feet cut off my sentence. The bullet sank into the earth by my shoe.

Self-preservation took over, and my body ran on instinct. I had to get away from the insane man with a gun. Over the quickened roar of my heartbeat, I heard his steps behind me. The air somehow choked me while simultaneously trying to rush from my chest. I ran until my legs ached before slowing to a stop. I wanted to curl up on myself and force the air back into my lungs as I doubled over and rested for a moment, but Vernon shot at the ground behind me.

Fucking maniac.

My feet pounded the ground as I kept running toward the tree line. Sweat fell from my temples and more gathered at my lower back, gluing the dress to my skin. I wanted to yell back at him, but my words were trapped beneath panicked and exhausted breathing.

Just as I reached the tree line, powerful arms engulfed me. I screamed out, and he put a hand over my mouth. I struggled in his grasp, trying to tug away from him. I was pissed. Even as the anger coursed through me, another emotion bubbled below the surface. I was enjoying his display of brute strength. And insanity.

He pushed me against the trunk of a giant maple tree. The bark's rough ridges dug into my back. He eased his hand away from my face.

"Are you out of your damn mind?" I yelled through heaving breaths.

He smiled. "Yes."

"You could have killed me! Get off me!" I strained against his immovable body.

I wanted Vernon, just not when I was panting and breathless from him shooting at me. But the way his strong arms held me weakened my resolve. The desire in his eyes lit up mine.

"Reaper isn't here to save you," he said with a grin that made me shiver even as his words excited me. "You're mine," he growled before kissing me.

I let his lips find mine in the greedy way I expected from Vernon, but his touch turned my desire to fear. He didn't realize his hunger for me triggered the memory from the alleyway all those years ago. Panic rose as he lifted my skirt up my thighs. I struggled to breathe as his buckle came undone, and then his cock was in front of me. I couldn't even speak. Words caught in my tightening throat as he lifted my thigh and pushed himself into me.

Pain. He was so damn big, even bigger than Reaper. It matched his stature. My lips parted to release a scream, but he threw his hand over my mouth again.

"Jesus," Vernon groaned as he pushed his hips into me, oblivious to the panic he sent ripping through me. The memories he accidentally forced me to confront. "Reaper was right. You feel fucking amazing." He leaned his face against my neck.

His hips pounded into me, making the bark rub my back raw. I strained against the hand over my mouth until tears slid down my cheeks. Tears I didn't mean to shed.

I didn't like to cry.

The moment the salty bead hit his hand, his head jerked away from my neck, his hard and crazed expression softened, and he stopped thrusting. He pulled his hand away from my face.

"Oh god," he said as he wiped a tear from my cheek. He twitched inside me. I think he enjoyed my tears, though he fought that enjoyment. "Sil . . ."

Sadness veiled the eyes looking back at me. Was it because he felt bad for hurting me or because he knew Reaper would kill him later? My heartbeat slowed and air began to leave my lungs more freely. My throat relaxed. The memories that haunted me receded into the back of my mind. I finally saw Vernon's game for what it was. Cat and mouse. A fucking stupid game, but a game, nonetheless.

His lips reached toward mine, and he took me into a passionate kiss I didn't expect from someone like him.

"I'm sorry," he whispered as he pulled away from me enough to get the words out. They were hard for him to say. Vernon didn't seem like the type who would apologize for anything, even something he did wrong. "I fuck women like I hate them," he explained as he pressed his forehead against mine, both so covered in sweat. "But I don't hate you." He kissed me again. "When they cried, it made me fuck them harder."

He twitched inside me again. I was torn between wanting him to get the hell off me and wanting to keep him inside me. His words melted me into the rough bark behind me. Instead of fucking me harder and ignoring my tears, he'd stopped himself. I hadn't known Vernon long, but I knew self-control wasn't his strength.

Vernon slipped the gun off his shoulder and let it fall to the grass. He pulled out of me and kept my thigh lifted as he dropped to his knees. I considered stopping him, but when his warm tongue hit my pussy, I forgot about the pain and fear he'd caused. I'd had a mouth on me one other time in my life, but it wasn't anything like this.

My eyes rolled back as I tilted my pelvis forward so he could lick me easier. I moaned as his tongue rolled up and down around my clit, exactly how I'd imagined it. I buried my hand in his dark hair. His free hand climbed my thigh and pushed inside me. His fingers sank deeper while his tongue curled across my clit. I gasped. He didn't care that I was sweaty from running. He tasted me like I was the best meal he'd ever had.

"I'm gonna come," I whispered, bucking my hips into his face.

I came against his mouth so hard that he had to catch me by my other thigh to keep me on my feet. He stood up, his mouth still sheening with my come, and kissed me again. I hesitated for a moment as his wet mouth spread my lips, letting his tongue find mine. I tasted myself. Sweet, with the salt of sweat.

His cock pressed against me as he kissed me. So hard and warm against my still twitching pussy. We didn't exchange words. Instead, he gripped his dick and pushed himself inside me again. Nothing except the weakened trembling of my thighs made me want to stop his driven, hungry thrusts. Even hungrier now that my taste coated his tongue.

He stopped thrusting and leaned into my neck, and a groan left his lips as he came. I'd never seen any man stop to come. It was as if he wanted my spasming pussy to finish him. He pulled out and caught his dripping come on the length of his dick. He rubbed it against my clit, making me jolt.

"Did Ricky tell you that I can't get pregnant?" I asked in a voice still laced with pleasure.

Vernon cocked his eyebrow. "No?"

"So you just came inside—"

"I'll always come inside you. You're mine," he said in such a cavalier tone as he tucked himself away and zipped up his pants.

The moment of sensitivity I saw in Vernon was gone. I knew it would be fleeting, but I wished it had stayed just a few moments longer.

He grabbed my arm and tugged me off the tree, and my legs shook beneath me as I walked.

Vernon reached behind me and rubbed my lower back. "I ripped the dress Reaper got you. He's going to kill me."

As pleasure continued coursing through my body like a drug, I didn't care.

Reaper met us at the door. His eyes went to Vernon before jumping to mine. My cheeks were still flushed. He looked at me like he knew something had happened, as if he could smell Vernon's come inside me.

"Did you fuck her?" Reaper asked. A twisted smile gave him the answer. Reaper circled me, assessing if I was okay. "I see you're in one piece," he said as he brushed pieces of bark from my hair. His hand reached out for the tear in my dress. "Really?" Reaper snarled toward Vernon.

Ricky walked between the two men and pushed Vernon, tugging the rifle off his massive shoulder. "You're a fucking fool!"

Reaper put his hand between the men and separated them. "What the hell's the matter?"

"Tell him, Vernon."

Vernon shrugged. "We were just playing around, is all. I wanted to teach her how to shoot."

Ricky turned toward Reaper. "I woke up to gunshots, and this fucker was shooting *at* her! Chased her off and shot at her!"

Reaper's gaze snapped to Vernon. "Is that true?"

"I . . ." Vernon started.

"I'm not asking you!" Reaper turned toward me. "Is it true? Did he shoot at you?"

I looked from Vernon to Reaper. My gaze finally dropped to Ricky, whose face was red with anger. I nodded.

Reaper took a deep breath and threw Vernon against the wall. "She's gracious enough to give us her body, and you have the gall to shoot at her?"

Vernon's eyes narrowed. "I wanted to catch her."

Reaper slammed him against the wall again. "If I ever hear about shit like that again, I'll fuckin' kill you. Do you understand? We don't shoot at broads. We especially don't shoot at ones we like."

I was frozen. I felt bad for Vernon getting in trouble, but he fucking deserved it. Even though he made me come, the events preceding the pleasure had been terrifying.

I was also stuck on the fact that Reaper said he liked me. It was a stupid thing to get caught up on, but my mama said I'd never find a man who would, and here I was . . . with two.

Ricky walked over and wrapped me in a tight embrace, squeezing me until he absorbed all the residual fear. He plucked another piece of bark from my hair. "You don't know what you got yourself into, love."

I didn't know what I was getting myself into, but a twisted part of me wanted to find out.

Chapter 8

"We gotta go!" Morris called out. He paced in front of the door and ran a hand through his hair.

Reaper tensed and looked out the window, drawing the ripped curtains aside. "There ain't nothing out there, Morris."

"The sheriff has driven by three times today. That isn't a coincidence. We've been here too long, and now we gotta leave."

I had almost dozed off with my head resting on Ricky's shoulder, but the moment Morris called out, the room changed. A rush of madness and mayhem engulfed us as we tried to get shit together.

"Go pack a bag, love. I think I saw a suitcase in the bedroom closet," Ricky said with a reassuring smile before getting up and grabbing his shotgun from beside the door.

I ran to the bedroom, adrenaline coursing through me. I expected it to excite me—it was excitement I had once daydreamed about while idly wiping the counter at the diner—but I felt like I would throw up with each knot of my stomach. Moonshine didn't taste good going down, and it sure seemed like it would be horrifying coming back up.

That's what I got for having more of their acrid booze with lunch.

I sat on the bed for a moment, trying to calm my nerves. Sweat beaded on my forehead, but I gathered enough strength to go to the closet, yank open the rickety door, and grab a small, dusty suitcase lying at the bottom. I picked it up and threw in the few dresses Reaper had purchased to replace the one Vernon ripped. I also threw in some slips and the couple nightshirts he picked up. That was all I really had.

Reaper showed up in the doorway as I fumbled with the snaps on the suitcase. His lips were tight. "You sure you wanna come with us? Last chance to back out, doll. We could drop you off some—"

"I'm sure," I interrupted, yelling over the protest of my belly.

Reaper smiled. "Fine, but take this." He stepped into me and slipped a small pistol into the palm of my hand.

I knew Vernon should have taught me how to use a damn pistol. I looked struck as I stared at him.

"Don't worry. It's loaded. All you have to do is pull the slide back and shoot. Hopefully, you won't need to. But some other gangs? They go for the women first. Take out what one man loves, and you crumble the rest."

I looked down at the pistol. "Where the hell am I going to put it?"

Reaper fished out a needle and thread kit from the nightstand. "Found this earlier. Your mama is a seamstress, right? Surely she taught you a thing or two. Use the old dress and make a pocket."

I hesitated before I took the items and sat on the bed. He left to help the guys gather their things and get them loaded into the car.

I struggled to thread the needle with my shaking fingers, but I finally got it. I stuck the needle into the mattress so I could rip some fabric away from the old dress. After removing my dress and turning it inside out, I sewed a pocket as best I could beneath the neckline, which would put the pistol right between my breasts. I didn't realize how poor of an excuse I was for a seamstress' daughter until I needed to sew a goddamn gun pocket. It looked like a child had done it, but when I put on the dress and tucked the pistol into the haphazard pocket, it worked well enough.

Through the open front door, I saw the men loading up the car behind an old barn. I walked out, and Morris came and took my bag, putting it beneath the seat with the rest of our stuff.

"Don't look so scared, sweets," he said, rubbing my cheek. "We do this all the time. That's the longest we've stayed in one place. The law isn't our friend, so we always gotta keep one step ahead of them. Reaper's wanted for murder. Vernon's wanted for . . . everything."

"And you?"

"The sheriffs want my real name. Morris is a ghost, and I'd like to keep it that way."

"And Ricky?"

"Golden boy. He's the only one who can lawfully go into town. Clean as a whistle. On the books, at least. The rest of us have to lurk in the shadows, but we've gotten real good at it."

Just as we were about to get into the car, a sheriff's car pulled up, kicking up dirt behind it. The driver and another man leapt out, guns drawn.

"We been lookin' for you boys!" the sheriff called out.

Ricky raised his empty hands. He'd already placed his shotgun in the car. Morris did the same, since his Thompson lay in the backseat.

The deputy stepped toward me and reached out, as if calling a hostage into the arms of awaiting safety. A brown mustache curled above his upper lip. I looked at the men.

Reaper's lips were tight. Vernon was fucking smiling. I met Reaper's eyes, and he tipped his head in a nearly imperceptible motion toward my chest.

I couldn't kill a man. I couldn't.

"Come on, darlin'," the man said as he encouraged me toward him again while keeping his gun trained on Vernon. "You're safe." Even as he reached out to me, his eyes weren't on me.

Ricky stepped forward, letting the sheriff preoccupy himself with someone to apprehend. He threw my angel to the ground. Ricky looked up at me with those blue eyes, and I knew what I had to do.

I nodded toward Reaper, and he slipped his hand up his side and beneath his jacket. I touched the front of my dress below the flushed red of my chest and gripped the pistol. In one fluid motion, I tugged it out, racked it, and fired right as Reaper drew his gun and shot the sheriff. The man in front of me—too close to miss—crumpled to the ground. Crimson spread around him as blood poured from his mouth. The dying man clutched his chest and released a horrifying gurgling sound. Reaper stepped closer and shot the man in the head, ending the suffering.

"Fuck, doll," Reaper said.

"We really gotta go now!" Morris called out.

I was frozen in place. The acrid scent of gunpowder barely registered in my stalled mind.

Ricky stood up and ran for me. He met my eyes by raising my chin. "You did so good, love." He leaned in and kissed me, and I kissed him back, letting it thaw my icy muscles. "We couldn't have gotten outta that without you. Well, it would've been more one-sided. Let's go." He grabbed my arm and tugged me toward the car.

Morris and Ricky sandwiched me between them in the backseat. Ricky ran his hand down my wrist and took the pistol from my trembling hand. He withdrew the magazine and racked it. The bullet in the chamber popped out, and Morris caught it. Ricky put the rogue bullet back into the magazine and loaded the gun once more.

"Just rack it again if you need to use it," he said as he handed it back to me.

My fingers didn't wrap around the metal. When I didn't make a move, he put it down the front of my dress, taking the opportunity to brush my chest as he did.

Morris' eyes hadn't left me. Actually, none of theirs had, except when Reaper was minding the road. Vernon wouldn't stop grinning. It was a smile that made me want to punch him. I'd just *murdered* a man, and he was grinning like a buffoon.

I should have been sick. I should have been vomiting up my guilt. Choked with disgust. But they surrounded me. They kept touching me and reassuring me that I made the right choice. I just wished it hadn't been the *only* choice.

I'd had another option, though. I could have left with the sheriff. I could have told them I was abducted. But that would have meant that the guys ended up dead or in jail. Reaper and Vernon wouldn't let themselves go to jail. They'd get themselves killed before they'd let the law catch them. Ricky was so innocent, and seeing him being captured . . . I had to be the devil to save my angel. My stomach tightened, nauseating me all over again.

"That was so goddamn beautiful, Sil," Vernon said as he turned to face me. He interrupted my panicked thoughts.

"You killed a lawman, sweets," Morris said as he grabbed my hand.

I inhaled sharply. "Oh god, I did, didn't I? Fuck."

Morris offered a warm smile that comforted me. "You sure did. There ain't no coming back from that. You're one of us now."

Before, I wasn't sure if I wanted to be *one of them,* but then the choice was made for me. I was one of them, whether I wanted to be or not. I was a *killer.* How the hell did I go from waitress to murderer after being around these four?

I was so goddamn confused. The way Ricky rubbed my thigh through my dress and Morris' fingers brushed the palm of my hand as he held it. The hunger in Reaper and Vernon's eyes. They confused the hell out of my body as I found myself more turned on than I should have been. That was the wrong response to killing someone. But I had killed *for* them. To protect them.

I realized what Ricky meant when he told me I didn't know what I was getting myself into. I was crawling toward darkness. And why did I love it?

I HAD FALLEN ASLEEP, my head on Morris' shoulder and one of my legs draped across Ricky's lap. He shook my leg as we pulled into another farmhouse. Darkness had blanketed the earth while I slept. Hours had passed, and we'd driven farther than I expected.

Loose boards crossed voids of emptiness on the caved-in barn, and the house didn't look much better. I sat up and looked out the window as Reaper drove on the grass and parked behind the barn. Well, what was left of it.

"We're gonna check it out. Wait with her," Reaper said to Ricky as the rest of them got out of the car. They crossed the lawn and continued down the small hill toward the house.

Ricky turned toward me. "You okay?" he asked.

I didn't know how to respond. I'd have been less upset if the man died on the spot, like how Reaper killed the sheriff. I struggled with the image of him sputtering out blood, aware he was dying.

"You are something else entirely, love," he said. "They don't make molls like you. They just don't."

I leaned into his comfort, his lips close to mine. He met my mouth and kissed me. It wasn't filled with the hunger of Reaper or the madness of Vernon. His kiss was soft and delicate. Sweet. He leaned over me and wrapped his hand around the back of my neck.

"I want to make you come," he whispered, asking for permission.

I didn't know the rules. I was with Vernon and Reaper. I was theirs. The last thing I wanted to do was piss them off.

"I can't." I shook my head.

"Why not?" he asked with a raise of his eyebrow.

"Reaper and Vernon."

"What about them? Because you've slept with them? Oh, love. We're pretty much brothers. We're family. I don't think they'd care."

"I'll talk to Reaper," I said.

He listened to my hands as I pushed him away, then he wiped his mouth and smiled. "Fair enough."

Was I really going to ask Reaper if I could have Ricky too? Three of them? I had to be stuck in some goddamn dream. A fantasy. But the memory of the murder still invaded my thoughts, reminding me of the reality of my situation. It was somehow a dream *and* a fucking nightmare.

Reaper opened the door and looked down at us. The flush in our cheeks shone red against our pale skin.

He cocked his head. "Come on," he said as he motioned toward the house. "Morris is trying to get the water working."

We carried our things inside—bags of money, suitcases, and guns. Lots of guns. No broken window waited above the door's aged wood this time.

"Ain't no one been here in a while," Reaper said as he entered the house. "All I had to do was shove, and it opened."

Looking around inside, I saw the pure abandonment of the place. Everything was in some form of broken. In the first room beyond the door, two sides of a cracked table leaned against each other. A couch—torn but relatively intact—waited inside the living room. I turned down a hall and went into the bedroom, where I found a derelict, well-used bed. Tears and holes in the mattress allowed its yellowed innards to poke through.

"Do you mind sharing this with me? I ain't taking one of the rooms with no bed, and you ain't sleeping on the floor." Reaper took off his shirt and laid it out on the bed. "You can sleep on this."

I smiled at him. I appreciated the gesture. "I don't need no special treatment just because I'm a woman."

"You ain't just a woman, doll. You're ours. And we take care of what's ours."

Chapter 9

I woke up with Reaper's arm around me. He slept on the bare mattress; the house was still in shambles. When I turned over, Reaper possessively tugged me into him. I had stirred too many times with nightmares that forced him awake as well. He just kept holding me every time I woke up with tears falling down my cheeks.

"Sorry I kept you up all night," I said, sleep still thick in my voice.

"The nightmares? They go away, doll. Once you do it again, you'll hardly feel a thing."

I scrunched my nose. "I don't want to do that again."

"You'll probably have to," he said with a tight smile. "We all have." He shifted onto his back and pulled out a cigar, lit it, and inhaled the smoke. "Once you went to bed last night, Ricky told me he kissed you."

"Oh." I swallowed and braced for his anger.

Reaper pulled me closer, and I dropped my head to his bare chest. The rhythmic beat of his heart thumped against my temple.

"If anyone deserves a broad like you, it's that one." Reaper blew a thick wave of smoke in front of my face, and his hand stroked the small of my back. "What do you want, doll? If you want all of us, you can have us."

I looked up at him. "How?"

He set his strong jaw. "We're family, and you're one of us. You can have anything I'm able to give you. If it's Ricky, or even Morris, then they're yours, too. But I won't give you up. I'm not willing to let you go. You can have whoever you want, but none of us ain't an option." He smirked as his hand roved down my back and grabbed my ass from beneath my nightshirt. "And if I want you, the others can fuckin' wait."

He growled as he put his cigar down, kissed me, and pulled me onto his lap. He was hard beneath me, and it lay against his taut stomach. I rubbed myself over his length, coating him with my wetness. He groaned as he reached up, pulled me down by my hair, and drew my lips to his. I kissed him and dropped my hands to the bed, holding myself over him. Reaching down, I guided him inside me. A deep growl vibrated his whole body as if he were electrified.

"Fuck," he whispered.

He stretched me as I rocked my hips on him. The hairs of his pelvis rubbed my clit as I grinded into his lap, and he gripped me with rough hands.

"I don't make love," he said before pulling out of me and laying me on my stomach beside him.

He got behind me and raised my hips. Pushing himself back inside me, he leaned over and fucked me with such intensity that I couldn't help but cry out. To stifle my screaming moans, I buried my face into the shirt he'd laid across the bed. The more I struggled to keep quiet, the harder he fucked me. He lifted me by my shoulders, put a hand over my mouth, and bit into my neck.

"Shh, doll. The others are sleeping." His fingers slipped

into my mouth, forcing it open and turning my screams into whimpers.

Reaper was a beast in bed. He was hard, fast, careless, and not as nice as he'd been the first time. The driven part of him —the part that made him suitable as a leader—made him push nearly through me with every thrust. Confidence radiated from him as he fucked me. Unable to take so much strength and tenacity after such a lengthy absence from a man, I nearly begged for him to stop.

I'd found myself with two of the toughest men I'd ever met, and they made sure I knew it. His fingers left my mouth and ran down my neck, strong and threatening, but I wasn't scared.

"If you're going to fuck her like that, at least make her come," Ricky said from the doorway.

I looked back at him. His sweet expression was playful, but his hard cock pressed against the front of his boxers.

"I'm sure you're better at that than me," Reaper said through clenched teeth. He released his hold on me, and I dropped back onto my elbows. I knew he was getting closer, but I could only bury my face into the soft white material of his shirt beneath me. "I'm not holding back, doll. Broads begged me to stop long before now." Reaper brushed a sweaty lock of hair from my cheek.

"I'm not like most broads," I said through the pain.

As much as it hurt, I didn't want him to stop. I wanted him to make me feel the pleasure, the pain, and everything in between. He released some of the power in his thrusts, as if he'd been testing me. The fraction he drew back was enough to stop the intense pain in the deepest part of me.

"You'll only make her prefer me once I make her come," Ricky said as he rubbed down the front of his boxers.

Reaper turned to look back at Ricky. "I'm fuckin' to release the tension of yesterday. I won't tell you how to fuck her. If she wanted something more, she'd tell me. Right, doll?" He pushed my hair aside to look me in the eyes.

I nodded. I didn't care if he made me come. I just loved feeling this small beneath him.

He pushed his frustration into me until he came, his thrusts finally slowing. His body pressed me against the mattress as he leaned over to kiss me, hard and gracious.

"I thought I was convinced before . . . but I'm so fucking convinced." He kissed me once more before climbing off me.

I stayed flat on my belly, panting for breath. The mattress dipped as someone sat beside me. An arm reached out and turned me over. It was Ricky. I couldn't take another dick. No way in hell. I ached as if Reaper was still inside me.

He pulled me into him and kissed me. "Told you he wouldn't care." His smile was still playful. He leaned over me and put his hand between my legs, and I jolted from his touch as he rubbed my clit. "Now can I make you come?"

He didn't wait for my answer. As he continued to rub me, I lifted my chest and let the pleasure creep from my pelvis to my very core. The pain from Reaper still radiated through my pussy, but the immense pleasure from Ricky's touch held it back. His mouth dropped to my neck and chest, kissing my flushed skin.

"Oh, angel," I moaned.

He lifted his head at my nickname for him. His hand snaked around my neck and pulled me into him.

"Come for me, love," he whispered against my mouth.

I trembled as my pleasure grew. He palmed me and rubbed until I came hard against his hand.

He kissed me once more. "I can't wait to have more of you."

Chapter 10

The sun's rays broke through the open window and crawled across the old wooden floors. I smoothed my dress over my hips. Morris showed up in the doorway, wearing a suit that was somehow still crisp despite all the mayhem. A fedora covered his dark hair.

"Here," he said as he walked toward me. He removed a box from his pocket and spread it open. Diamond earrings glimmered against the sunlight. "Do you like them?" he asked.

I fought back a gloss that began to overcome my vision. I'd never had something like that. "I'm tearing up because I *love* them," I said as I took the box. My fingers grazed over the prongs holding the diamonds. "They're beautiful." I couldn't help but wonder where he'd gotten such an expensive pair of earrings. Were they stolen from someone who loved them as much as I did?

"I'm glad, sweets. We're going to meet with the head of the Italian mafia."

"Are the others coming?"

Morris laughed. "Nah. I can't bring them along for something like this. We need permission—the graces—to get some more moonshine stills going in this area. Reaper is too threatening. Vernon makes people uncomfortable. Ricky hates bootlegging." He smiled. "Plus, I look like I got my shit together walking in with someone who looks like you."

My cheeks flushed with heat. Morris reached out and adjusted the clip in my hair, letting a few strands fall loose.

"Let's get going," I said as I tore my gaze away from the mesmerizing gray of his eyes.

We walked toward the front door, passing the living room.

"Wait!" Reaper called out. His deep voice stopped me in my tracks. He got off the old, ratty couch and dropped on one knee in front of me. I put my hand on his head to balance myself as he pushed up the skirt of my dress.

"Uh . . ." I teetered as he pulled my leg forward and ran his hand along my inner thigh. "Can I help you?"

He looked up at me from the ground. "They'll check you and Morris for a pistol, but they wouldn't check between your legs, doll." Reaper put my pocket pistol against my inner thigh and taped it to my skin with medical tape. His hand went higher until he grazed my pussy, making me jolt. He smiled and tugged my skirt down again. "If things go south, just aim and fire. There's a round in the chamber." Reaper got to his feet and stared down Morris. "Don't let anything happen to her."

WE DROVE toward the city until roads finally began to look familiar to me. The car slid past my mama's seamstress business, and my eyes followed the sun-faded awning in front of the building. I searched for her through the windows.

"Does she know where I am? Or that I'm even alive?"

"She knows you're safe, but we can't tell her where you are, and neither can you."

I nodded. I understood. When we drove by, I expected to feel a sense of longing to go home. Instead, I only felt an urge to get as far away as we could.

We continued on and eventually passed the diner. The "open" sign in the window glared back at me. I never wanted to step foot in that place again, but my feet were stepping in worse things with Reaper and the gang. Things like blood and violence.

I dropped my head against the headrest with a sigh. I should have *wanted* that boring and regular life back, but a nagging feeling in my gut told me I could never go back to the way things were before I met them. I was being seduced by the lifestyle—by the men.

Winding roads led us to a big mansion on a hill. We pulled up to the front and were greeted by men with guns. I lifted my hands as one turned his rifle on Morris.

"We have a meeting," Morris said, his hands still firm on the wheel.

The man with the rifle looked at the other man and nodded. We got out of the car under their watchful eyes, which scanned me until a bright blush rose into my cheeks.

One man threw his gun over his shoulder and searched Morris. His hands prodded beneath his armpits, his hips, and even his ankles. The other man threw his rifle behind him and circled me. I dropped my hands to my sides and tried to stop the sweat from gathering on my forehead. I struggled to keep my breathing calm as his hands grazed my body, slowly and sensually. They traced down my armpits, brushing against my sides as he lowered them further. They rode over my hips before slipping backward and grabbing my ass. I flinched at his touch and looked over at Morris. His cheeks flamed with anger.

"Do you need to check her like that? She doesn't have anything on her," he said.

My breaths hitched for a moment as the man's hand slid toward my inner thigh.

"That's enough," the other man said, and the one behind me withdrew his hand. I exhaled.

Fuck, that was too close.

They guided us inside, and we stepped into a smoke-filled room where men were laughing and drinking. The strong scent of patchouli and vanilla floated through the smoke, almost overpowering the stale nicotine aroma. Morris reached out and grabbed my hand. He squeezed it.

One of the men leaned against the table. He dominated the room, clearly the boss. His eyes met mine, and smoke blew out from around a cigar in his mouth.

"I didn't expect you to bring company, Mr. Morris," the man said as he pushed off the table.

"She's my wife." Morris tugged me into him.

"She is stunning," the man said. He stepped into me, lifted my hand to his mouth, and kissed the back of it. "Pleasure."

"All mine," I purred.

"Have a drink, you two," he said as he grabbed glasses from the cabinet and filled them with real alcohol. Not just moonshine, but golden liquor that made my mouth water.

I swirled the glass, let the oaky perfume wash over me, and took a sip. It hit my throat and soothed it instead of burning it. Morris looped his arm in mine and tugged me toward an open pair of seats. I sat down carefully, trying to keep the pistol from pinching my skin. The tape snatched at my tender flesh.

"How many did you say you wanted?" the man asked.

"We'd like to operate three, maybe four stills," Morris replied. "Locally operated. We just need your graces, sir."

"I appreciate that you come for my permission. Some of

you think we won't find out, but nothing happens in or around this city without me knowing. How many do you run with?"

"Three others."

"That's less than I expected." The man squelched his cigar in the ashtray. "Two stills seem more workable with that amount of men, no?"

"We don't want to be involved with bootlegging exclusively. Just a little here and there," Morris said as he leaned forward. "Two would be reasonable."

"With two stills, you can sell to any of my speakeasies, as long as it's just product from those two farms." He leaned over and grabbed a pen and paper. "These two aren't manned at this time. The farms are in the middle of fucking nowhere, which is farther than my men want to deal with. Your group is welcome to them. Thirty percent comes back to us. Another ten goes to the farmer."

Morris nodded. "Fair."

The man handed Morris the paper, and he tucked it inside his breast pocket.

"I'll give you a free still if you want to give her up for the night," the man said with a smirk as his eyes dragged down my body.

Morris' cheeks pulsed as his jaw set. I squeezed his hand.

"She isn't for sale," Morris said, trying to control the temper in his tone.

"Shame."

"Thank you, sir, for your generosity," Morris said through his clenched jaw as he stood.

The man and Morris shook hands, and Morris grabbed my arm. His cheeks were still pulsing as we got into the car. He put the car in drive and pressed the gas pedal to the floor, kicking up dust behind us as he sped off. Tension rippled through the car.

When we got back on the road that would lead us to our current safe house, Morris pulled over and turned toward me.

"Fuck him. The way they put their hands on you." Morris shook his head. "He had the nerve to ask me for a night with you? He's lucky I didn't kill him for that. You don't ask another man if you can sleep with his wife. For a fucking still?"

"Morris," I said, trying to calm him down and stop the rush of words leaving his mouth.

While he trembled with anger, I leaned into him and kissed him. It's all I could think to do to pull him back into the moment. As my lips touched his, he forgot about everything around us.

"Oh, sweets." He groaned against my mouth and leaned over me, running his hand up my thigh. He snatched off the tape, pulled the gun away from my inner thigh, and set it on the dashboard as he kissed my neck. "I want you," he whispered against my skin.

"We can't stay on the road, Morris," I said through panting breaths.

He hesitated before pulling away from me and adjusting himself as he got back behind the wheel. "You're right." He put the car in drive, and we took off toward home.

We pulled up at the farm, the car hidden again by the dilapidated barn. Ricky was the first to greet us. He put his face in his hands as he looked me up and down. He wiped at the lipstick smeared on my face from Morris' kiss. Ricky's gaze jumped to Morris.

"Please tell me this was from you?" Ricky said.

"Yeah, it's from me." Morris wiped at his own mouth. "That fuck asked for a night with her, though. Fucking prick."

"He did what?" Reaper asked from the doorway.

"Yeah, said he'd give us a free still for a night with her," Morris snarled.

"He's fucking lucky I wasn't there," Reaper said.

Warmth washed through me. I felt so protected and safe.

Mosquitos from the swamps behind the house gathered around my legs and bit at them. I swatted the relentless pests away. "Can we go inside?"

Even once we were back in the house, insects still flew in through the cracks in the door's splintered wood.

Vernon caught a moth with his bare hand and crushed it. "How'd it go?"

"Got two stills. She got a goddamn proposition," Morris said with a sneer.

Vernon cocked his head.

"I guess he wanted a night with our girl," Reaper said.

Vernon smiled at me. "Who wouldn't? Can't blame him."

"Fuck him." Morris waved Vernon off as he shrugged out of his jacket.

Reaper kissed my head. The moment his strong arms wrapped around me, all the nerves from the day were drawn from me and into him. I was falling hard for them. I craved the touch of each man.

Reaper's strength.

Vernon's crazy.

Ricky's sweetness.

And Morris was somehow a mixture of them all.

Chapter 11

I picked at the food on my plate as I looked around the kitchen. Half of everything was ripped out and being tinkered with since the men were trying to make this place habitable . . . for a while, at least. Roots from a tree beside the house somehow snaked through the cracks in the walls, as if nature had begun to reclaim the building. The fireplace was black with soot, and a lone pot lay overturned inside. At least Morris had gotten the water going, which was what mattered to me.

I yawned. I didn't sleep much the night before because an owl kept hooting by the window, which was cracked just enough to let the usually beautiful sound travel straight to me. My nerves also kept me up. Going to meet that big city fella, with all his money and men, had excited me.

I'd been a cog in the machine of their operation, even if I was only playing a part. I had no idea how much they'd let me into that side of things. It wasn't that they didn't think I could handle it, but I worried they wanted to shelter and protect me. I had no interest in being sheltered anymore. I lived my entire life thinking there was little else beyond my walls. As it turned out, there was a whole big world. Their world. An exciting and dangerous existence that made me appreciate every new day.

I finished the food they left for me and, with a stifled yawn, I headed toward the living room. Reaper, Vernon, and Morris had gone off to secure the stills, but Ricky wanted nothing to do with that. He sat at a small table in front of the couch, playing solitaire. He moved his hand along the lines of cards laid out in front of him, his top teeth biting into his lower lip with focus. He looked up at me and smiled.

"You wanna play?" he asked.

"No, I'll watch." I was too tired to focus on the rules of another game.

I sat beside him and laid my head in his lap. He brushed my hair back and kept his hand on my shoulder.

"How can I focus on playing with you right there?" he said with a smirk.

The way he looked at me sent a feather drifting around in my stomach.

A grandfather clock ticked in the corner of the room. It had been broken, too, but Morris got it working again. It kept the room filled with rhythmic ticks and melodic reminders of the lapses in time.

When Ricky finished his game of solitaire, he gathered the cards in a pile and set them on the table. A smile slid across his face. "Come with me," he said as he stood and grabbed my hand.

He led me toward my bedroom. When he opened the rickety door, an array of colors filled the room. Beautiful spring flowers. Their gentle, earthy perfume masked the musty smell of the abandoned house. I looked at Ricky with a slack jaw. No one had ever done something so thoughtful for me.

"It isn't much, but—"

"No, it's so much, angel."

He pulled me into his arms and kissed me. "I couldn't wait to get you alone, love."

"Why'd you wait to finish playing your game, then?"

"Had to get my nerves up. Playing helps."

He lay back on the bed and tugged me over him. My slip rode up my thighs as I dropped my lips to his. I thought I was dreaming. I questioned my reality. How was I on the lap of someone as handsome as Ricky? He was perfect, and the unhurried way his hands moved down my body made me feel like I was perfect, too. He absorbed every bit of me, as if committing me to memory.

His hands finally landed on my ass, and a growl simmered in his throat. His hand reached down, unzipped his slacks, and revealed his cock. It wasn't as big as Reaper's or Vernon's, but it had a perfect curve that made me want to find out how it'd fill me.

"I know I'm not like the others. They may be able to fuck you harder, but I can fuck you differently," he said as he flashed his blue eyes at me.

Reaper and Vernon lit a fire in me that I risked the flame for. Even when it burned me, it was the pain I wanted to feel. Ricky would fuck me no better or worse, just differently. He'd foster and harbor a controlled blaze, burning off all that was wrong with me and leaving all that was right.

I lowered myself onto him. He groaned as I sank lower on his lap, as if he'd been thinking of this moment since I first walked in the door and made him drop the glass in his hand. I moaned and dropped my face against his neck. He smelled so pure and clean—different from everyone else. And in so many ways, he was.

Ricky raised his hips to meet mine. I pressed my chest against his, his work shirt rubbing against my skin. I rocked my hips on his, and his hands rose up my arms before he put my head between them. Loose hair fell in front of my face. He pulled me in for another kiss, unhurried but just as filled with desire, as if he were savoring my mouth.

"Love," he growled against my lips, "you feel even better than they say you do."

I throbbed at his words and the lust which followed them. I sat up, letting my hair drape down my back. Sweat covered me and dripped from the tips of my hair. A warm bead of it slid down the small of my back, leaving goosebumps in its path.

I put my hands on his chest as I rode him. I couldn't stop looking at him. He put his hands on my hips, looking up at me with the same fondness. Ricky had a way of making me feel loved, really loved, with just a cast of his light eyes. It was different.

His top teeth bit into his lower lip and sweat trickled down his temples.

I yanked down the straps on my shoulders, freeing my breasts from the heat beneath the fabric. He groaned at the sight before letting his hands ride up, leaving a smeared path of sweat from my hips to my chest. He grabbed my breasts with both hands, a low groan leaving his lips. He smirked at me as he let one hand fall between us. His thumb caressed my clit, side to side between my legs. I dropped my head back.

His touch was amazing, but it was his entire being that fed the storm brewing inside me. The way he looked at me, like I was the most important thing in his world at that moment. It was also the curve of his dick inside me, riding along the natural curve of my pussy, and his hand making waves between my legs. All of him created a tsunami within me.

My thighs quivered. His fingers thrummed my nipple. Pleasure coursed through me until it took over my body. I moaned as I captured his mouth again.

"Angel," I whispered against his lips.

"You are perfect, love. So damn stunning."

His compliments against my mouth made me shiver. I felt so loved.

He swirled his finger around my clit and made me come hard, squeezing the pleasure from him as well. He groaned as he nipped into the soft skin of my shoulder. He twitched inside me as my spasms embraced him.

He was everything I didn't know I needed.

As we rode the coattails of our orgasms beside each other, Vernon appeared in the doorway. It startled me to see his quiet figure standing there, staring at us. I expected his face to be twisted in jealousy—maybe even anger—but instead, he looked almost proud.

"Are you going to stop obsessing over her now?" Vernon said to Ricky with a laugh.

Our cheeks flushed red. I covered mine to hide my shyness.

"Nope. If anything, I'll obsess a bit more," Ricky said as he tugged me into him. "She's real easy to love."

"None of us are easy to love." Vernon scoffed. "That's why we're family."

Vernon was right. We all had our baggage. Our demons that made us unlovable.

For me, my demon was thinking a man could never love me if I couldn't give him children in return. That I was somehow less of a woman. Maybe even deserved to be alone, serving others instead of making a home. For Reaper, it was mistrust. With Morris, it was whoever he was before he gave himself a new name. Ricky was plagued by the path of his brother. And Vernon? Well, even his demons had demons.

Chapter 12

Rainwater dripped down the speakeasy walls. The wide alleyway behind it boomed with sound—murmurs of men, strained shouting for final bets, and the patter of shoes on wet concrete.

I rubbed my arms to chase away the cold chill from the damp air. Morris shrugged out of his jacket and draped it over my shoulders. I smiled at him, and his gray eyes bore into mine. I dropped my gaze at his intensity. I felt the same desire he had.

I looked back at the makeshift ring, paint sloppily laid out in a circle. I didn't quite understand why we were there or why all these people were there. I knew Vernon said he was a street fighter, but I didn't think he meant fighting in the actual street.

Anxiety grew in my gut as the tension in the crowd shifted and became heavier. Vernon cracked his neck before stepping into the circle. Another man, much shorter but equally as muscular, stepped in after him. A bell rang and I expected a fight like Reaper and Vernon had demonstrated at home. It was nothing like that. The men immediately clashed.

Their bodies were a heap of brute force. There was no reservation in Vernon's punches as he laid them on the other man.

I covered my mouth so I wouldn't feel tempted to call out. I knew Vernon was violent, but seeing it in person, in front of my very eyes, was . . . a lot. There was no inhibition in his strength as he cut up under the man's ribs with a nauseating sound.

Flesh on flesh.

Screams and grunts.

"How are you guys so calm?" I asked, wringing my fingers in front of me.

Morris leaned in and kissed my forehead. "Don't worry, sweets. Vernon lives for this." He smirked. "And he never loses."

His words comforted me a little. Vernon did look happier than a pig in shit in that ring. Even when he took punches, his inappropriate smile remained.

A cold raindrop hit my cheek, and I wiped it away. I looked back at the others, who looked hungry for the fight. They'd bet on Vernon, and each swing of his meaty fists got them closer to winning.

Vernon's balled hand flew forward and made contact with the man's face. He stumbled before falling onto his back. Vernon leapt on him, straddling his hips. Relentless punches followed, each one leaving the man's face more and more twisted and unrecognizable. Vernon didn't stop. He just kept drawing his arm back and doing it over and over until the beaten thing beneath him hardly looked human. His grunts were something I'd never heard as he released his frustration and anger through his bloodied fist.

A referee—who should have stopped it before now—rang the bell. When Vernon didn't stop, he stepped beside him and rang it louder. Vernon finally grounded himself, lowering his fist and clambering off the man. Only once Vernon got to his feet did I see all the blood marring his skin.

Reaper and the others celebrated the victory. I handed Morris his jacket before they went and gathered their winnings. Street fighting was a blood sport, and Vernon wore that crimson proudly.

I leaned against the wall and smoked a cigarette. Vernon came up beside me, startling me as I brought it to my mouth again. Just as I wrapped my lips around it, he caught it, snatched it away, and took a deep drag. The cherry glowed and sizzled against the blanket of night.

"Come," Vernon commanded as he dragged me around the corner of the building, away from everyone.

He slammed me against the wall of the speakeasy. There was no one around us. No sounds except for Vernon's heavy breathing. His eyes were crazed, still riding the high of the fight.

"Sil, does me almost killing that man make you afraid of me?" He twisted a lock of my hair in his hand.

I swallowed hard. Did it? Not as much as it probably should have.

"I'm fucked up. I'm a bad fucking person. I couldn't care less about taking someone's life." Vernon pushed his knee between my thighs and spread them. "I'm not gonna shoot at you this time."

He released a sadistic laugh that almost made me want to scream out for the others. I stifled it. He put his hand beneath my dress, and his bloody fingers raced up my thigh. The sticky trail of blood chilled my skin. His arm hooked around my thigh and lifted my leg. With his other hand, he worked down his pants as his mouth found mine, leaving a metallic taste along my tongue.

Part of me wanted to stop him. The rest of me wanted him to keep going.

"Does the blood make you want me to stop? Or does it make your pussy wet?" Vernon asked. His hand rode up further, palming me, his rough fingers sliding along my slick skin. "Fucking wet," he said with a growl.

Vernon moved his hand away and gripped his cock, stroking it a few times before leaning into me. I whimpered as he rubbed the warmth of his dick against me. He covered my mouth with his massive hand, and blood spread across my face as he leaned closer to my ear.

"Shh, Sil."

When he shushed me, memories flooded me until I was drowning. The dripping water off the building behind us. The alleyway. Rough thrusts. The scent of steam rising from the pavement after the rain. Being unable to scream. The snarling *shh* of the man who caused me such pain.

Tears fell, and I had no control over them. I reached out to push him away, but he still rubbed himself against me. He leaned further into me before he noticed I was crying. Probably thinking something was wrong with me, he stopped the movement of his hips and cocked his head. He tugged his hand away, and I leaned against him with panting, panic-laced breaths. He didn't hug me or comfort me. Instead, he stood there, confused as hell. His hand left my thigh, his cock hard in front of me as he backed up.

"It's not you . . ." I finally said as my heart returned to a normal rhythm.

"You don't cry with Reaper," he said.

"It's *how* you go to fuck me." When he just stared at me as he tucked himself away, I continued. "I was raped in an alley like this. It was a lifetime ago, but that made it feel like yesterday."

Vernon's expression softened a bit. His eyes rounded, but his lips tightened. He trembled with anger, but it looked like he was just shivering from the cool night air.

"What the hell happened?" Reaper said as he turned the corner, nearly knocking into Vernon's steadfast body. He looked at my blotchy face, my tears taking in the moonlight on my cheeks. He pushed Vernon away from me, pinning him against the wall. "What'd you do to her?"

"He didn't do anything," I said as I tried to get between them—which was incredibly stupid.

Vernon drew his arm back, ready to hit Reaper, but I grabbed his wrist and made a last-ditch attempt to put myself in the line of fire.

"Stop!" I pleaded with them. I'd have to admit what I told Vernon if I had any chance of making them stop. "I told him about how I was assaulted in an alley like this. That's why I was crying. He didn't do a damn thing!"

Reaper's hard eyes narrowed. "He did. He probably tried to fuck you like the goddamn animal he is."

I went quiet. Vernon was selfish and hungry, and that was clearly who he was, but so was Reaper. He could have triggered that memory just as easily, but it happened to be the perfect place, the right hand, and the wrong person. Vernon wasn't the man who assaulted me, even if he was the embodiment of what that person was—selfish and opportunistic. But Vernon didn't *want* to hurt me. He didn't want to destroy me. He just wanted to be inside me.

Reaper released Vernon and focused his attention on me. With still-hardened eyes, he pulled a pocket square out and wiped at my face, trying to get rid of the blood. "I appreciate you not shooting at her this time, but you're still putting her at risk out here. After a fuckin' fight. With all the men around. If something happened to her . . ."

Vernon's jaw clenched, as if he was really holding back what he wanted to say. "I wouldn't let *anything* happen to her. You aren't the only one who likes her, you know. I just have a shit way of showing it." He pushed past Reaper and disappeared around the corner.

Neither of them showed their feelings the same way. Reaper showed it through his fierce protectiveness, like the way he defended me from one of the most important people in his life. And Vernon? He showed it by being a little less of who he was.

I didn't need any of them to change for me, though. Each of them filled a void I had, including Vernon. Maybe even especially him.

Chapter 13

The wind blew my hair back as we drove. It was just me and Morris again, on our way to meet an arms dealer this time. Morris needed to call me his wife again, just to thwart suspicion. Our contact asked to meet in the middle of nowhere, so Morris and I dressed in our best and began the drive. It seemed suspicious as hell to me. Part of me wondered if it was all a ruse concocted by Morris to get me away from the others. That part of me hoped I was right.

Every so often, Morris would glance sideways at me, and my heart would stumble over a beat. He hadn't tried to sleep with me since our last outing. It'd only been a few days since we asked for the stills, but it felt like forever. I thought there was something heating up between us, but then he got cold.

I watched the trees as we drove, just starting to grow their leaves, trying to hide the branches which laced across the sky. Birds dotted the clouds and flapped wings that raced against the wind. Other birds huddled on the branches, waiting out the gusts.

"Can I ask you something?"

He cocked his head. "What's on your mind, sweets?"

You. That's what I wanted to say, but I chickened out and pivoted the conversation. "Would you ever tell me your real name?"

Morris chuckled. "Nah. Not in this lifetime. You wouldn't like me too much if you knew who I really was."

"Who said I liked you?" I smirked at him.

"You're right. Presumptuous of me." The corners of his lips turned down.

"Presume away," I said as I reached out and put my hand on his thigh.

I gained courage at the worst time—just as we pulled into an open field where another car waited. I leaned forward to look out the windshield. A man in a long, dark coat stood beside his car. He wore a hat with a low brim that concealed his eyes. It made my heart beat faster.

"Wait here, sweets. If anything goes south, slide over and get the hell out of here, okay?" He smiled at me before climbing out of the car and making his way toward the other man.

I watched Morris walk. Calm and confident. Safe. Which was precisely why he didn't bring the others.

"Who's she?" the man asked, gesturing toward me.

"My wife," Morris responded, as evenly as he could. He tucked his thumbs into his pockets and stood taller.

Now I knew it was a ruse. My presence did nothing to help the cause. If anything, it raised more suspicion.

The man went to his car and pulled out a big rifle while keeping his wary eyes on me. He handed the gun to Morris, whose arms lowered as the weight of it sank into them. It looked heavier than the others I'd seen them use. Morris checked to see if it was loaded before raising it so he could look down the sights. His finger curled around the trigger and squeezed, dry firing it. Morris passed the rifle back to the man and pulled out a wad of money. He slipped him at least a couple hundred, maybe more. The man handed over the rifle, and the deal was done.

Morris came back to the car and put the rifle in the rear floorboard. "Vernon's gonna need to carry that thing. It's twenty pounds unloaded. I'll keep my Tommy."

"What is it?" I asked, not that it made much of a difference to me.

"BAR. It's an automatic and a fucking beast."

Morris got in the car, and we watched the other man drive off. Dirt kicked up as he sped away.

Under the weight of a tense silence, it was time to ask him why things felt so stagnant between us. "Morris—"

He interrupted me with a kiss. His hat slipped off his head and fell behind him as he leaned over me. "I know what you're gonna ask," Morris said with a smirk that I felt against my lips. "Just wasn't the right time, is all. I knew I'd know when it was. Calling you my wife does something to me, sweets."

Not waiting for my response, he kissed me again. I slipped further down the bench seat until my head lay against the sticky leather. Morris crawled over me. His fingers grazed my cheek before his hand ran down my neck. He lifted my skirt, letting it spill over my stomach. One hand grazed my chest through my dress. His fingers rolled over the curves of my breasts while his other hand worked down his slacks.

I couldn't see what his cock looked like beneath the excess fabric between us, so I dropped my head back and let myself feel it instead. He pushed inside me. His groan vibrated the walls of the car, as if I felt like everything he imagined. I moaned as he pushed himself further. He wasn't as big as Reaper or Vernon, not as thick as Ricky, but he filled the very depths of me as he drove his hips into mine.

The leather seat pinched at my bare skin, warm and sticky from the sun, but I didn't care. I could only focus on his hands, which didn't seem to know where he wanted to grab. He wanted all of it. All of me.

"Is this real, Morris?" I asked through heavy breaths.

He lifted his gray eyes, and I swallowed hard. "I can ask you the same thing," he said as he kissed down my neck. "I feel so goddamn lucky."

I moaned as his pelvis tilted and he curled his hips into me. Morris kept one leg down on the floor beneath the wheel as he sat up on his other, perched on the bench with me. He looked uncomfortable. His hand reached between my legs, and his fingers rubbed me.

"Let me get on top of you," I whispered.

He cocked his head and smiled before we adjusted ourselves. As he sat down, I finally got a view of his cock. Every curve and arch of him was familiar already.

I tugged my dress over my head, sweat making everything stick to me. I kept my slip on. The thin fabric was nothing compared to the dress. I crawled over his lap and tugged down my straps until my breasts came free from the fabric. Morris growled as his hands met them. He squeezed the flesh until I moaned at his tame roughness, somehow a mixture of all the men, just like his personality.

It was almost stern.

I lowered myself onto his lap, and neither of us cared if my come stained his slacks. I wrapped my arms around his neck and pressed my chest against him as the sun shone through the windshield, warming my back and flushing my skin further.

I rocked my hips on him. My face dropped into his neck. "You still won't tell me your real name?" I asked, my cheek buried against his shoulder.

"Not even a moll like you could get that outta me," he said with an upward thrust that made me jolt. "The others have been trying for years." He fisted my hair and made me look at him. "It's really better you don't know." He kissed me. "Now come so I can finally feel what they brag about."

I grinded my pelvis on his lap. Sweat gathered at the base of my spine where my back curved, and I rode out my pleasure. His hand dropped from my hair and moved toward my ass. He squeezed as he guided my movement. I was so damn close, filled with so much more than his dick.

I felt happy.

Loved.

He made me come, and I spasmed. My entire body trembled as I came around him. He groaned as I twitched on his lap.

"My girl," he growled as he came, slowing my motion with a firm grasp on my hip. "You're even more than they bragged about."

I climbed off him and lay down, trying to calm my trembling body. I let the pleasure ripple through me until it died. Morris smirked at me before throwing the car into drive and taking us toward home. I leaned my back against the door, curling my knees toward my chest as his come dripped from me and stained the hem of my slip.

Morris glanced at me. "Keep showing me that and I'm gonna have to pull over again, sweets."

I clenched my thighs together with a playful smile and leaned my head back, letting the wind play in my hair. I half expected to wake up from a dream, certain this wasn't my reality and it was all something I made up. I'd open my eyes and be back in the shitty diner.

We pulled up to the house and got out. Morris grabbed the BAR, and I grabbed my dress. The door slammed behind me once we got inside.

Reaper's eyes roved up and down my body. Morris shook his head and passed us. Reaper stood from the couch and turned me around, running his hand along my ass. He lifted the back of my slip, his fingers going to the spot which was wet with come.

He cocked his head. "What's all this, doll?" He tugged me into him with a strong grasp I couldn't pull away from. He bit my neck. "Did you enjoy yourself? Is it your come too?"

I dropped my head to the side, letting him devour more of my neck. "Yes," I said. "It's mine too."

"One day I'll stop being so stubborn and make you come, doll. I ain't jealous of any of them, but I wish I was more of what you need. But that's what they're for. They can give you more than I can. Different things than I can."

The way Reaper bit into me made sure I knew just how real it all was. This wasn't a dream. It was my new life, and I'd been reborn.

Chapter 14

"Wanna go for a walk?" Ricky asked as he slung his jacket over the couch. He unbuttoned his dress shirt and pulled it off, leaving only his undershirt and the nice dark slacks.

I shifted my weight on the cushion of the couch. A walk? It seemed so mundane. Something so simple that didn't really seem to fit in the chaotic life I now lived.

"I . . . I don't know."

"Just say yes," he said with a smile as he gave me his hand.

I followed him outside, the door slamming behind us. We walked along a field that reminded me of the one I ran across when Vernon shot at me. Grass tickled my ankles as we walked further away from the old broken-down house we'd tried to make a home.

We sat in an area of flattened grass.

"I come here most days," he said.

"Where'd you grow up?" I drew my knees toward my chest, the breeze playing with my hair.

"Philly."

"Such a short answer," I said with a hint of sadness. I wanted to know more about him, about any of them.

He smirked. "It's all you asked, love."

Fair, I guess. Each man was as tight-lipped about his past as the next one. I thought if anyone would be more willing to give me some of his history, it'd be Ricky.

He lay back with a sigh, putting his hands behind his head. I lay beside him, and we stayed silent for several minutes, with only the whistle of the breeze around us.

"I was born in Philly and moved to New York with my brother when I was twenty," he finally said. "He got caught up in the outlaw lifestyle, and I got wrapped up in it by being the brother of an outlaw. No matter how much I tried to stay away, it was like a blackness creeping toward me until it took over my body and mind. That's why I hoped you'd leave, as much as I wanted you to stay around."

"You didn't think I'd be able to fit in with you guys?"

"Oh, love." He kissed my forehead. "I knew you could run with us, but I didn't think it was a good idea. You aren't the type to become black hearted like us. I still have bits of my light left, unlike the others. Vernon and Reaper have hearts as dark as their souls. They got soft spots for you, though. Morris . . . you wouldn't know what he was like on the inside. None of us do. But I think you got a lot of life in you still. Things you can become that aren't this." He gestured toward the farmhouse.

Ricky was so goddamn sweet. Almost too sweet, like you might get sick from how much of him you ate. Grass tickled the backs of my arms and legs as we lay in the field together, and Ricky stroked my hair as I curled into him. The sun warmed me, and I closed my eyes to soak it all in. I still saw the red-hot light from behind my eyelids.

"I got nothing else back there, angel. Light as I may be, I want to be within the dark."

"You got your mama."

"Yeah, a woman who made me feel like a failure for years because I can't be a mother. I don't miss being told how lonely I'll be until the day I die."

"Men care that much about babies?" Ricky asked, a hint of laughter in his tone.

I played with his undershirt, toying with it nervously between my fingers. "As if it's their life's purpose to plant their seed."

"Well, it doesn't matter to me or any of us." Ricky pulled me toward him and kissed me. "This isn't really the lifestyle for little ones."

"You guys won't ever settle down? Want families?"

"Once you've done the things we've done, there's no settling down. No room for family. Life will always be unsettled, and we'll always try to keep one step ahead of the law. I could probably settle down if I left right now. I haven't become the face of this gang. Not yet." He flashed his blue eyes at me. "But where would I go? I got everything I need here. The guys. You. My family. Do you think I could get a moll like you on my own? A guy like me wouldn't be enough for you."

His words wrapped me in a familiar sadness that I'd felt for as long as I could remember. Not that I was worthless, just that I had *less* worth. Ricky was perfect exactly how he was. If asked who I'd marry, it'd probably be him. But I wasn't willing to choose.

"You would most definitely be enough," I purred against his ear.

He smiled before kissing me again. His warm hand rode up my cheek and slipped behind the sweaty curve of my neck. He climbed over me and spread my legs with his knee, his lips never leaving mine.

Ricky let go of my neck and placed my head on the soft grass beneath me. His hand slid down my side and gathered my skirt, tugging it up. He unzipped his slacks with the other hand, letting his cock fall from the fabric. He leaned over me and kissed me again. The heat of his cock hung between my legs as he rubbed me.

"I won't last long with you, love. I'm going to get you close before I fuck you," he said against my mouth. His lips left mine, and he kissed down my chest to the swells of my breasts. "God, you are so perfect."

I closed my eyes as he rubbed my clit with a firm but gentle touch, swirling his fingers around me with a selfless hunger, like he was living to make me come at that moment. Every so often, he'd reach down and give a long stroke of his dick, fending off the ache he had for me.

My back arched as he pushed his fingers inside me before rubbing me until I was a slick mess that would invite him inside me. I lifted my chest, and he looked down at me with his stunning blue eyes.

"You gonna come, love?" he asked.

I nodded, though I was sure he could feel it within every tight and tense muscle in my body. He could hear it in the moans I tried to keep at bay. He had to know.

Ricky stroked himself once more before leaning forward and pushing himself inside me. We both groaned at the same time, as if our bodies had been waiting for that single moment with tense anticipation. He kissed me, stifling my moans as he thrust, slow and sweet and exactly how I knew he'd fuck me. One hand laced behind my neck again while the other reached between my legs to rub me. I was so close to the edge, pushed even closer by the feeling of his cock inside me.

Pleasure swarmed me in an almost overwhelming feeling of warmth and happiness. It wasn't just from the sun shining down on us and heating our bodies. It was from inside me.

I reached behind him and gripped his shirt as I lifted my chest to his. I bit my lip to try to stifle the moans, but they were persistent. I came, shuddering against him, riding out an orgasm I had never felt before.

"I'm coming, love," he said as he dropped his face into my neck. Pleasure saturated his soft groans. "I told you, I couldn't fuck you like they do, but I'd fuck you differently." He smiled again and kissed me.

Chapter 15

Vernon, Reaper, and Morris took me with them to check out the still about an hour north of us. With Morris beside me, Reaper fucking me with his eyes through the rearview mirror, and Vernon turning around every so often to stare at me, that hour went by real quick. My heart felt so full. The only one missing was Ricky. He still wanted nothing to do with the bootlegging part of our operation. He tried to convince me to stay behind with him, but I needed to go. Not even the prospect of another incredible orgasm from his selfless touch could keep me back.

Vernon turned once more to look at me. His eyes didn't roam over my body with their usual rabid hunger. He looked at me with something more, his jaw tense and set. It was almost worse.

We hadn't talked much since the night I told him what happened to me, and I felt rejected by him. Reaper also knew, but all he did was fuck me like he needed to protect me more. My cheeks blazed hot before I looked away from his burning gaze. It was as if he didn't know what to say to me. Or how to say whatever it was he thought he needed to say.

Morris tugged me into him, and I rested my head on his shoulder. I needed that so much at that moment, and it was like he knew that before I did.

"It's okay, sweets," he whispered against the top of my head.

Gravel rumbled beneath the tires as we pulled onto the long driveway that led up to the farmhouse. Paint peeled from the barn's metal walls, but at least it stood in one piece, unlike the dilapidated excuse beside our current safe house. The harsh sun beat down on the barn's tin roof, and heat shimmer radiated off the metal.

Vernon's attention snapped to the farmhouse. His eyes scanned the surroundings. "Something doesn't feel right, Reaper," he said as he lifted his shoulders.

I looked around, trying to understand what he meant. A bit of raised dust lingered in the stagnant air outside the car as we pulled up, but that's all I noticed.

When the car stopped, Vernon and Reaper got out. Morris leaned into me before following them.

"Wait here," he said with a squeeze of my hand.

He tucked his pistol behind his back, and the three men walked toward the farmhouse. They stepped around the front of the place, peering into the barn before coming back to the car. Morris opened the door for me, and I slid out.

"There ain't nothin' here. Not even the farmer," Reaper said.

Vernon didn't relax as we walked to the barn door. It was cracked open, so he gave it a push to get a visual on the condition of the still. That was all we needed.

A disgruntled looking chicken rushed from behind the door, releasing a blast of angry clucks as it ran off and scared everyone half to death. I understood why *I* was scared, but these were mobsters—men who shouldn't be scared of some scrawny bird. I almost let out a laugh, but I heard something else inside. Was it another barnyard animal?

"Long way away from the city, folks," came a voice from just beyond the door.

Reaper drew his pistol from its holster, but the subtle *click* behind him made him stop.

Vernon's cheeks throbbed as the man appeared from the barn's shadows. He was nicely dressed, but not nearly as nice as my men. His eyes moved over my body, twisting my stomach into knots of discomfort. Aside from the pulse of his cheeks, Vernon kept still as a statue, his hand in his pocket.

Morris stepped forward, getting between me and the man. "Clearly there's been a misunderstanding," Morris said, calm and confident. His soothing voice could sell meat to a butcher.

"Nope." The man shrugged. "I think I'm being quite understood. We want this still."

I swallowed hard. There were only two of them, and they were pretty ballsy to take us on. If I were them, I'd have hidden in the shadows until we left.

The man tapped his shoe against the rusty metal still. It was clear what he wanted, but that wasn't the deal Morris and I made with the Italians.

Vernon and Reaper exchanged glances as the man continued to prod at the still. Reaper was still trying to reason with the man, but it grew increasingly hard to hear over my heartbeat thumping against my eardrums.

Morris reached his hand back and tapped the butt of his gun before dropping it to his side once more. I took a step forward, and Morris put his hand around my waist. I wrapped my hand around him, and he tugged me into him. No one seemed to notice us. I clutched the grip of his pistol. It was much bigger than mine, and its bulk filled my grasp. I yanked it from behind Morris' back, keeping my eyes ahead of me, on the man who stepped closer and closer to Reaper.

He really wasn't far away—maybe ten feet, positioned between Vernon and Reaper in my line of sight. I took a deep breath. I had one chance to do this, and while they'd started teaching me to use the pistol, I still didn't feel experienced enough to make the shot and not hit one of my own.

Morris turned his head just enough to look at me. His gray eyes were dark and pleading. He gave me the confidence to do what I needed to do.

Time seemed to slow as I drew the pistol, hoping like hell it was already racked. I aimed and squeezed the trigger. A loud explosion of noise burst from the silver barrel of Morris' gun and echoed around us.

The man behind Reaper slumped over and fell to the ground. Reaper didn't waste a moment as he lifted the hand still wrapped around his pistol and shot the man by the still as he reached for his gun. Vernon tugged the knife from his pocket and leapt on the man on the ground. Reaper kicked the pistol out of his trembling hand, and Vernon screamed as he buried his knife into the man. There was so much blood, I couldn't tell if it came from the hole in his side or the rip through his abdomen.

Vernon grabbed the man by the hair, craned back his head, and slit his throat. He had to saw through the flesh and tissue, producing a slow, nauseating sound I'd remember until the day I died. The jagged skin spread as the man clutched his throat, somehow still alive. His mouth opened as he tried to take a panicked breath.

"For fuck's sake," Vernon snarled. He got up, took the gun from my trembling hand, and put another bullet in his head. Only then did the man on the ground stop moving. Stop gurgling. Stop breathing.

Vernon took a breath like he didn't just murder that man.

A calm, relaxed breath that made him seem almost soothed by it. Though I wasn't as upset this time, I still struggled to calm the panic in my chest. It had to be done, but when the adrenaline stopped coursing through my veins, the nightmares would creep over me once more.

"Morris, help me with the bodies," Reaper commanded.

Morris shot me a smile before helping Reaper move the bloody corpses toward the field.

Vernon put the pistol behind his back, tucking it down his slacks. He pulled me into the barn and tugged the door partially closed to hide the blood trail on the floor. My eyes scanned his body. Blood coated his shirt and hands. He was covered in it. The metallic scent washed over me. His eyes were hard. That rabid hunger I said he was missing? He found it. He found all of it.

His hand wrapped around my neck and slowly dragged down my throat. He rubbed his thumb along my lower lip, and I smelled the blood on his hand as he touched me. He pushed me against the wall of the barn, and the hot metal warmed my back. I was still horrified that I'd killed yet another man, but Vernon couldn't keep his hands off me.

"That's twice you saved our asses, Sil," he said through clenched teeth, as if it took everything in him to hold himself back.

His hand slid down, squeezing roughly when he passed the notch of my hip. I flinched at the harsh touch, and he reined it in, controlling something deep within him. He patted my hip where my skin still tingled from his firm grasp.

"The things I've done to others? I'm not supposed to do that to you," he said through a shallow inhale. "But I know you'd love me, even if I did."

I sucked in a breath, and my heart caught in my chest at his words. He was right. Even when he shot at me or triggered my memories, I wanted more of him. I would still love him. I couldn't imagine what Vernon had done to others, but if it was anything like what he did to other men . . . well, I'd be in for it. I already knew he liked to play cat and mouse games.

He cast his dark eyes on me and kept them locked on mine as he balled up the fabric of my skirt and lifted my thigh. My mind swirled. The scent of death hung around us, and Vernon wore its paint on his skin, but I had to see where this went.

His touch was heavy but gentle, rushed but sure as he kissed me, and I forgot all about what happened and the situation we were just in.

"I'm willing to be someone other than myself because I'm falling too damn hard for you, Sil."

His hand felt like fire on the back of my thigh as he held up my leg. He reached down, unzipped his pants, and pulled himself out. I prayed to God I wouldn't freak out on him again, but with my nerves raw and my mind racing, how could I not?

He silenced my thoughts with his mouth. He pulled away long enough to spit on his hand, rub himself, and push inside me. I inhaled a sharp breath. He made a move to put his hand around my mouth again, but he stopped, as if remembering the night in the alleyway. His hand fell from my face and went to my neck as he used a kiss to silence me instead.

"Vernon," I said through a low moan.

He pulled back. "No one has ever looked at me with such fear and . . . something else. Something fucking else entirely." He marked every word with a rough thrust.

He stilled his thrusts but not his hips, grinding circles against me. I choked back a moan as his pelvis rubbed against my clit. His words electrified me, awakening every nerve in my body. I looked up at him and pulled him in for another kiss.

"You don't look at me like I'm broken," I whispered against his mouth.

Vernon drew away from me and smirked. His eyebrow raised. "Broken? You're the least broke of all of us."

I wished that was true. I was broken, just in different ways and in different places.

"We ain't doing this here," Reaper said from behind Vernon.

I'd been too wrapped up in Vernon's greedy thrusts to hear them enter the barn. I thought for sure I'd hear the squeal of the rusted door as they opened it.

Vernon turned his gaze to Reaper. His voice was deep and menacing in a way I'd never heard him talk to our leader. "I'm finishing this. I need to finish this." His words softened as they came from his mouth. It was as if he needed to prove something to me. That he wasn't going to do what he did before.

Reaper threw his hands up. Vernon's roaring demon meant it wasn't the time to fight it. Instead of leaving, Reaper waited. He bent his leg, leaned his foot against the doorway, lit a cigar, and smoked.

Several seconds passed before I could focus my attention back on Vernon. I still couldn't believe they were so comfortable around each other. Around all of this. Even as Vernon leaned into my neck and fucked me harder, I didn't believe it.

The leg I stood on quivered from exhaustion and pleasure. Feeling how I trembled, Vernon lifted me and wrapped my legs around his waist. I moaned into his bloody shirt as he took me against the wall in ways I didn't think possible with him—without a single intrusive memory, not even of what just happened.

"You feel so incredible," I whispered.

"You have no idea what you do to me," he growled. "How hard you make me all the goddamn time." He kissed me.

His words pushed me closer to the edge, but there was no

way I could come. Not like that. Not with the scent of death around us.

He halted all movement of his hips and came inside me with a gravelly groan that made me shiver. Reaper puffed his cigar, masking the scent of blood as he tugged me from Vernon's grasp and smoothed my skirt.

"Real fuckin' stupid," Reaper said to Vernon, shooting him a glare that would kill if it could. "You don't know how to act around her. I don't trust you not to hurt her."

"I would never hurt her," Vernon said as he zipped up his slacks. "I know I'm not who you want me to be for her. I know that. But I'm fucking trying, Reaper." His voice revealed a hint of desperation at the end. He was trying to prove he could be something different from what he'd always been to me and Reaper. But mostly, he was trying to prove it to himself.

Chapter 16

A knock on the door made us leap from our skins. None of us liked the idea of someone coming unannounced. Reaper dropped his hand to his pistol as he stood, and Morris kept his on the Thompson.

"Who is it?" Reaper called through the old door.

"Chet, looking for Ricky."

Reaper looked back as Ricky stood and went to the door. His face didn't show any signs of recognition. Reaper covered Ricky as he opened the door. Now there was some recognition on Ricky's face.

"I remember you," Ricky said as he leaned against the door. "You ran with my brother for a while, right?"

The man nodded. "I need a place to lay low for a few days. Everyone's dead."

"I . . . I don't . . ." Ricky stammered as he looked back. "Be right back." He closed the door.

"Who is he?" Reaper asked.

"Chet, I guess? I didn't even know his name, but he ran with my brother before he came to you guys. Says his gang is dead. Needs somewhere to lay low for a few days."

Reaper sucked his teeth. "Normally, I'd help. People have taken me in at my worst. But with Sil here—"

"Absolutely not," Morris interrupted. "We aren't housing some wayward mobster with her here."

Reaper rubbed his chin. His eyes glanced from me to Ricky and back. He pushed Ricky aside and tugged open the door. "A few days. Max. Enough time for you to get your bearings and get going."

Reaper turned away from the heavyset man. His deep-seated eyes looked untrustworthy to me.

Reaper gestured toward me. "One thing needs to be crystal fuckin' clear. She's our moll. You are not to touch her, look at her, or even breathe wrong around her. Do we understand?"

Morris scoffed and defensively pulled me into him. "We won't leave you alone, sweets." He kissed my head as Reaper welcomed the guy into our home.

My safe place.

I was uneasy as fuck about the whole thing, but what could I do about it?

I LAY on the couch with my head in Ricky's lap and my legs stretched over Morris. Ricky brushed his fingers through my hair while Morris rubbed my calves. They were talking about the stills, and Ricky's disapproval painted his expression.

Every time I looked up, the man in the chair across the room stared at me. Stared at *us*. He looked like a starved animal. I half expected a pile of drool beneath his chair when he stood up.

When he got to his feet and left the room, I sat up, pulling my legs off Morris. I turned toward Ricky and leaned close to his ear.

"How long is that guy staying?" I asked.

Ricky shrugged.

He'd only met Chet a few times, but he didn't really get to know him. The odd man didn't seem like the "get to know people" type. He offered us money to stay for a few days. That's all it was supposed to be, but he'd been breathing our air for nearly a week.

Even when he told us his name, I didn't trust it. Something about his eyes nurtured an uneasy feeling in the pit of my stomach. I knew I wasn't the only one, because my men hovered around me, just like Morris promised. Reaper didn't leave me alone, even in bed at night. He'd let the others handle business while he kept himself present. His pistol always remained visible on his side. When Ricky and Morris were home, Vernon and Reaper would scurry off to have business conversations—things I didn't need to be in the know about, which was fine with me.

Chet kept paying, and I was starting to learn how to live around him by avoiding his creepy fucking staring. He frequently brushed back his sandy hair and offered me a rough nod, and I wasn't sure what the hell that meant. He'd only said two dozen words since he'd been here, crashing on the couch at night.

"Where you from, Chet?" I asked as he sat down with a glass of moonshine.

When he saw the man staring, Morris tugged down the bit of my dress that had ridden up my thigh.

"Somewhere," Chet said before taking a long sip of his drink.

I tightened my lips. Morris was a mysterious man, but Chet was just weird. He gave me the creeps. Chet looked straight ahead and ignored us as he took gulp after gulp of shine. He scratched beneath his suspenders, snapping them as he stopped scratching.

"I have to piss," Ricky said.

His eyes met Morris', and I knew what they were saying without saying anything. Ricky got up, hesitated for a moment, and went to the bathroom. Morris wrapped his arm around me.

Chet got up and strolled toward the couch to sit beside me. Morris tensed. He was reading the room, taking it all in, and he liked none of it.

"You fuck them all?" Chet asked me, his breath heavy with moonshine. He leaned over and twirled a strand of my hair.

I narrowed my eyes at him.

"Don't touch her," Morris commanded. I'd never heard him raise his voice like that.

"Don't be like that. If she's the gang's moll—"

"She isn't the gang's moll. She's *our* moll," Morris said with a deepening tone.

Chet reached for my thigh with a laugh and mumbled something about sharing me, but I could hardly hear it over the explosion of movement and sound around me.

Morris leapt up and pushed Chet away from me. "Get your fucking hands off her!"

"What the hell is going on?" Reaper asked as he came into the room. Morris never really yelled, so it was no surprise that it caught Reaper's attention.

Morris had his hands at Chet's chest. Chet was too big to throw his weight around, but he knew it and used it.

"Let go of him," Reaper said.

Morris hesitated, pushing further into Chet's chest before releasing.

Chet's laugh turned my stomach. "I just wanted a little bite of her," he said with a smile.

"Do you have a suicide wish?" Morris snarled at the man.

"I'm fine." He sang the words as he threw his hands up.

Morris took a step back to let him get off the couch. Chet's breath was heavy with alcohol as he pivoted his body at the last moment and let his hands touch the bare skin of my thighs.

I screamed.

Before I could even register what happened, Reaper had drawn his gun, cocked it, grabbed Chet's head, and shot him through the throat, careful to send the bullet upward as it blazed a path through the man's skull. Fragments of brain matter showered the wall and couch. I covered my mouth as a spray of red splattered onto me, painting my cheek.

Blood oozed from the man's open throat and dripped onto the front of my dress, between my breasts. Before meeting these men, I'd never seen a man die. Now I'd seen five, and this one had collapsed on my lap. I'd never seen the insides of someone's head so close, yet there it was, pretty much sitting beside me on the couch. Blood seeped into the beige fabric, staining it a deep brown.

I screamed out and flailed beneath the body.

Vernon came running at my screams. He cocked his head at Reaper, and his eyes jumped to Morris, whose face flushed with anger. Ricky ran in, zipping up his pants as he did. His eyes went wide.

"He tried to touch her," Reaper said with a sneer.

Vernon narrowed his eyes at the bleeding man on my lap.

"Can someone *please* get him off me!" I yelled.

Vernon grabbed the man beneath his armpits and lifted him off my lap as if he'd just picked up a sack of potatoes. He dropped him to the ground, and blood pooled on the wooden floors.

Vernon's eyes were on me. A gross smile crossed his face as he grabbed my arm and helped me to my feet. He kissed me, pulling away long enough to let his tongue lick the blood from my cheek. "You okay, Sil?"

"I told you he was a creep!" I yelled out. I pulled off my dress, exposing the blood which had saturated through to my slip. Another line of blood curved across the top of my cleavage and fell between my breasts.

When I looked at each one of them, they were hard. Reaper and Vernon didn't hide their erections—or their stares. Ricky clasped his hands over his lap, trying to hide his. Morris adjusted his slacks, trying to get the pressure off his dick while looking away.

Vernon licked his lips, his eyes glued to my chest as if he wanted to lick the rest of me clean.

"Did he touch you?" Reaper asked. He stepped into me, holstered his pistol, and grabbed me by my shoulders.

When I didn't respond, he shook me. I met his eyes and shook my head. He didn't really get far, and I wasn't sure the quick grope was worth a bullet, no matter how creepy he was.

"I'll kill a man for far less than that," Reaper assured me.

It still felt *wrong*.

Vernon shrugged. "I was probably going to kill him anyway."

Morris came up behind me, grabbed a piece of . . . something . . . from my hair, and tossed it aside. My stomach tightened.

"I'm sorry," he whispered in my ear.

How could I blame them for the dead man on the floor? I killed the deputy in colder blood than that. I shivered. I was no better.

"Look at me, doll!" Reaper commanded, shaking me back from the memories of the lawman.

My eyes found his.

"You see this?" He grabbed my chin and forced me to look at Chet's body once more. "This is what we are. What we do.

You've seen what we are. You've lived amongst it. I ain't ever lied to you about it. I told you to leave. I *wanted* you to leave." Reaper swallowed. "But now I don't want you to go. None of us do."

They all shook their heads.

"You need to decide what *you* want. What you'll accept. You can take one of us, all of us, or none of us. If you don't want us, I'll let you—"

Vernon interrupted him with a scoff.

Reaper snapped his attention to him. "*We'd* let you go," he snarled at Vernon before turning back to me. "I promised you no one would hurt you, and I intend to keep that promise." He raised his chin. "What do you want, doll?"

"I..."

I didn't know.

My eyes leapt to each of them, including the dead man on the floor. My hesitation made the usually composed Reaper drop his shoulders. Vernon looked fucking pissed and I hadn't even made my decision. Morris and Ricky kept out of it, but their postures showed how invested they were in what I'd decide.

I looked back at Reaper. His normally hard eyes were sad. It was the first time I'd seen that emotion from him, and I thought he was incapable of feeling anything besides the hunger for something he wanted to devour or steal.

"I'm gonna regret this," I said, mimicking Reaper as if I had a gun drawn on him.

Reaper pulled me into him and hugged me, and Ricky and Morris smiled as they joined in. Vernon pushed them aside and picked me up, wrapping my legs around him and licking the blood off my chest.

With Reaper's threat still lingering in my memory, I looked over at him. "Don't make me fucking regret this."

Men of Vengeance

Chapter 1

September 2nd, 1932

Being a moll wasn't for the faint of heart, but baby, I wasn't for the faint of heart. I never thought that I'd be here with them over a year later. I also didn't expect to become such a part of their lifestyle.

Didn't expect to fit so perfectly.

I became the strong and brave woman who always brewed beneath my surface. I became all that with the support of my men... my family.

I lay entwined at the waist with Reaper, a cigarette between my fingers. Smoke billowed from beside me. His real name lingered on my tongue. It was so damn hard not to say it when he was fucking me just right, which he always did. No one could call him Robert, not even me.

My fingers grazed the soft, dark hairs of his chest. Sometimes I forgot just how dangerous he was, but you don't get the nickname "Reaper" from being no saint. Reaper didn't carry a scythe. No, he preferred that dark Colt revolver that never left the holster at his side. Even when I fucked him, that pistol dug into my skin.

The door swung open and Ricky ran in, a towel around

his waist. I squealed as his wet blond hair sprayed everywhere, like a puppy coming in after a storm. I called Ricky "angel" because the boy was a fucking angel. This lifestyle absorbed him much like it had absorbed me—against our wills in our own ways. When I looked at him, I didn't see how he fit in with them, but he was every bit a part of them.

The same thing could have been said about me. Thick, wavy auburn hair that grazed my shoulders, the greenest eyes, and a soul that was becoming blacker by the day. That's the only thing that was growing black. My heart was still so full of love that there was no room for darkness to creep in.

I knew Ricky's heart still had some light too. He wasn't like the rest, and I never wanted him to be. The only thing I wished I could change about him was his growing hesitation to pull the trigger, which was no good. I always told him, shoot first and cry about it later. Ain't no time for a conscience when staring down the barrel of a gun.

I looked over at Reaper lying on his back and smoking a cigar. His cheeks puffed as he inhaled the thick smoke and exhaled it into the air around us. He seemed unbothered by Ricky's antics as he lay naked, his spent cock limp against his thigh.

Hands raced over my naked body, and I melted into the touch. My angel. My sweet boy. He kissed my neck, his lips falling to my skin so gently that it felt like the wings of a butterfly against me.

Reaper would never fuck me like Ricky, and I didn't want him to. I needed Reaper for what he was, and I wanted Ricky for what he wasn't. He wasn't a hardened killer like the others.

Ricky climbed between my legs, unbothered by the come of our leader inside me. He kissed me, brushing my hair back with soft fingers. I reached down and spread his towel, and he wasted no time in drawing my legs apart with his knees and pushing himself inside me. There wasn't a lick of hesitation as he pushed past Reaper's come and planned to mark me with his own.

Reaper put out his cigar in the tray by the bed and turned toward us, a sly grin on his face. "You two have fun now, because we ain't staying here," he said as he rubbed his strong hand, scarred and dangerous, down the fragile curve of my neck. I'd seen what he'd done with those hands. Snapped necks much stronger than mine. Despite the danger when within his grasp, I knew he'd never hurt me.

I moaned at the touch of them both on my body. Reaper gave me a smack on the cheek and climbed out of bed, leaving a silent longing where his body once lay.

Ricky grabbed my attention with his mouth again, tugging my lower lip between his teeth. He curled his hips into me, the soft and gentle thrusts so characteristic of him but so uncharacteristic of what we were. Droplets of water dripped onto my chest from his shaggy blond hair and fell between my breasts. I shivered despite the heat of Ricky above me.

"You are incredible, love," he purred against my cheek.

If it were me in the crossfires, Ricky wouldn't hesitate even half a heartbeat to save me. He'd get the strongest feelings of them all and have no shame in showing it. I didn't mind one bit.

I brushed my hand through his hair. "I'm sick of being beneath you boys," I said with a smirk.

He met the upturn of my hips with his and rolled off me. I crawled over him, straddling his lap and guiding him back inside me. His hands reached for my chest, caressing my nipples with a feathery touch. His blue eyes looked up at me with nothing less than love, and I returned those same feelings. As I grinded my hips on his, I remembered the day he first saw me. I walked in and the kid dropped the glass he was holding, just like in the movies. He looked at me the same way now, just without the glass shattering all over the floor.

He pulled me into him, wrapping his arms around my back, which was damp with sweat. His hips met mine halfway. I touched my forehead to his, and his soft groans nestled between my ears, where they'd live forever. Well, as long as *we* lived. He wanted to come. I knew he did. The muscles in his arms flexed, tensing as his grasp around me tightened. I also knew he'd fight the fuck out of it to get me off first.

"Don't worry about me, angel. Just come for me," I whispered against his mouth as I kissed him.

"Silvia," he groaned.

"Just come," I said more firmly. I took control of the motions to push him over the edge. I wanted him to feel good. We all needed to feel good before shit hit the fan again.

His hands dropped to my hips, and he rode out his orgasm, his lip twisting as he came. He groaned against my neck, dripping with sweat. I rolled off and lay beside him. My sigh was heavy and full of pleasure. It didn't matter if I came or not. The rest of it was enough for me.

A year ago, I had wondered what I was to them. I knew I was a toy to play with. One they didn't intend to pick up in the first place. I had been collateral. In no time, they let me in as much as I let them in. I became *their* moll. There was never jealousy. Never anything between us but love.

When new guys would show up to do a small stint with our group before they either ran off or got killed, my family was furiously possessive of me. I wasn't the *gang's* girl. I was *their* girl, not to be shared by anyone else who joined. Reaper killed men in front of me for thinking I could be shared. Their blood would splatter against my skin as their bodies fell to the ground with hard cocks. You'd think that would make me scared of him, but it only made me love him even more than the minute before.

Did I ever worry if that was all I was to them? Never. They

killed too many times in my honor. They wouldn't have done that if I was just a place to warm their cocks at night.

I rubbed my fingers through the blond hairs on Ricky's chest. He blew out a thick exhale and pulled me into him, drawing me out of the current of memories trying to suck me under.

"We really doing this tomorrow?" Ricky asked.

The robbery? Oh yes. We weren't being stupid about it. We planned to rob an armored truck, with cash upon cash inside, all protected by one or two simple men with simple guns. We didn't have quite the gall to walk in the front door like some gangs. The less our faces showed around the city, the better.

"It'll be fine. Reaper could do a robbery like that in his sleep," I said, comforting him.

That's one thing that was difficult with Ricky. The deeper we got into the lifestyle, the more timid he seemed and the more fierce I became. He was never the aggressor. That was fine for everyday life—if he'd been a husband or a father—but it didn't mesh well with the life we lived. If I had to make a bet, I'd lay a stake on Ricky being the first of our group to lose their life, and I fought heat between my eyes about it. Not my angel. He had to toughen up or they'd home in on his weakness like a fly to the dead.

"We'll be fine, okay?" I grabbed his face and drew it to mine. I couldn't promise anything, but I needed him to take a breath of comfort for a moment.

He nodded as he dragged himself from under my arm and out of bed.

"No, stay with me," I pleaded. I didn't want him to go off and wallow in his worry any more tonight. I'd remind him that safety was with me, and as long as I was there, he'd never be alone, even facing the cold embrace of death.

Chapter 2

The sun rose and blinded me through the bare, dirty windows. I slammed the curtains closed as I finished getting dressed, and ran my hands along my hips to smooth my skirt. I grabbed my small pistol off the dresser and shoved it into the pocket near my thigh. I was as much of an equal as any of the men in our group, except I had to do it all in a goddamn dress. That made me a bit tougher, I'd say.

I walked into the living room of the uninhabited home we'd seized for the last couple of nights. We weren't sure when the owners were coming home, and all of us were itching to get out of there before they returned. None of us enjoyed the idea of killing innocents, not even Reaper. The boys were all dressed and ready to go. They looked at me like I was the one holding them up. I probably was.

"About time, Sil," came a gruff voice from the corner of the room.

I flashed a smile at Vernon. He stood and placed his hat on his head and slid his pistol into a vest pocket. I never learned much more about Vernon or his past. He was as tight-lipped as ever about that. I did learn that his name wasn't no nickname. It was his pop's name, and he wore it proudly.

He walked over and took me into his arms. He kissed me with lips that spit venom. He was everything my mama warned me about growing up. Tall, dark, and handsome. He was as crazy as he was beautiful, and there wasn't an ounce of fear in that man's body. He'd be the first out of the car to face any opposition. His heart beat for this life. Sometimes I forgot he was even mortal, that he wasn't some god on the earth just for me.

Vernon released my face, and I let my eyes fall on the final member of my little family. Morris, who would take his real name to the grave before he'd tell any of us, even me. I walked over to him, and he pulled me onto his lap. His hands met my cheeks, and he squeezed them.

"Morning, sweets," he whispered. He was playful, but not like Ricky was. He was tough, but not like Reaper. He balanced us all out.

"Ready?" Reaper asked as he ran a rag down the length of his Thompson.

Vernon grabbed his BAR and let it hang loose at his side. Ricky twisted his sawed-off shotgun nervously. I felt for my pistol, which was all I carried into these things.

We piled into the car. I was sandwiched between the thick body of Reaper and the squirrelly thin body of Ricky.

"Can I have a cigarette?" I asked Morris.

He drew one from his pocket and lit it for me. I stared at his mouth as he puffed on it. A hint of flirtation sparked between us as his fingers grazed mine when he handed it to me. Yeah, he'd fuck the shit out of me when this was all over. Actually, both he and Vernon would. They lived for the adrenaline. I expected that of Vernon, but Morris transformed. I wondered if he'd finally let his guard down enough to show us the real him, even if it had a different name.

We pulled to the side of a long road heading toward the city. Vernon put the car in park and killed the engine.

I looked around. "You sure they come through here?"

"Questioning my intel, doll?" Reaper grabbed my chin.

I shook my head.

The boys got out of the car and got behind it, checking their watches as they sank beside the vehicle. I crawled into the driver's seat.

We waited.

It felt like forever, with nothing but smoke billowing up from beside me to pay attention to. I tapped my fingers on the steering wheel before leaning out the open window.

"Guys—" As soon as I began to question it, the truck appeared on the horizon. Dust rose behind it as it got closer.

I ran a finger along my lips to ensure none of my lipstick was smeared on my pale skin. I waved out the window at the driver of the truck. My heart thrummed in my chest as the truck pulled over. A man in a uniform hopped out of the passenger side and walked over to me, sending heat creeping across my chest. I steadied my breathing.

"Are you okay, miss?"

My eyes locked on the pistol he had on his hip. I ran a hand along my thigh and comforted myself with the touch of my gun. I pouted my lips. "Yeah, my car is just on the fritz." I flashed my green eyes up at him and twirled my red locks around my fingers.

I watched in the rearview mirror as Vernon snuck around the back of the car, which meant Morris was rounding the front. Morris popped up, drawing his pistol from his shoulder holster and aiming it at the passenger. In complete unison, Vernon leapt up and aimed his BAR at the driver. Neither had time to draw their weapons, so they raised their hands instead.

"Please, miss! I got kids," the passenger pleaded with me. I was the only one without a gun trained on them.

"Get down on the goddamn ground," Reaper said as he twisted the man's arm, coercing him down to his knees.

Tears flowed down the man's cheeks as he sobbed. The driver was much calmer, as if it wasn't his first rodeo. He didn't make a move for his gun, and not even a muscle twitched. Ricky ran to the back of the truck and started filling bags of money. With Reaper manning the passenger and Vernon covering the driver, Morris ran off to help Ricky. We had this robbery shit perfected to the point that it was as natural as the act of breathing. We knew our roles, and we got shit done. If we could keep things as clean as that, we'd be unstoppable.

Reaper hit the passenger with the butt of his gun, knocking him unconscious. Vernon told the driver to drive. The moment he sped off, my men hopped back in the car. The masculine tension within those metal walls made it hard for me to take a breath. Vernon howled in excitement as he dug through one of the bags.

"Oh fuck, sweets," Morris said as he pulled me in for a kiss. I tried to keep my eyes on the road as his hand dropped between my legs.

I batted his greedy hand away. "I gotta drive."

"Yeah, yeah. There won't be no excuses once we get you home," he said with a sly smile. I knew there wouldn't be. I was in for it with Morris and Vernon, and I was aching as much as I was nervous. Vernon wasn't gentle. Nothing about that man was kind. Or sane.

Reaper gave me directions to a farmhouse just north of the city. Gravel crunched beneath the tires, dirt rising around the car as we pulled up to the home. Overgrown grass choked the property, slowly taking over the walkway toward the house. There was a hollowness to the home, an eerie creak of emptiness. Even though it didn't look like anyone was home—or had been here in a while—we went toward the front steps with our guns drawn to be sure. Ricky plucked a weathered newspaper from the porch. More than a few weeks had passed since the date on the front page.

Reaper used the butt of his Thompson to break the door's glass window. Shards spread at our feet as he tugged it back and cleared the frame of any remaining slivers. He slipped his hand through and unlocked the door. Glass crunched beneath us as we headed inside. The boys did a thorough pass of the home, ensuring we were all safe there, at least for the time being.

I wiped sweat off my brow as the heat of the day dripped down the small of my back. I pulled off my dress but left my slip on. I sat on a dusty wooden chair and fanned my face.

"Don't bother cooling off, sweets," Morris said with a low growl. He picked me up and carried me, knocking me into the wall in his frustrated haste. "Where's the bedroom in this dump?" he called back to Reaper, who gestured down the hall. He carried me to the bedroom and tossed me onto the bed. Dust plumed around us, becoming one with the stale air.

My eyes jumped to the cracked window beside the bed. A glass vase and dead rose sat on the sill. The dry, crunchy petals gripped the stem by sheer willpower. If I reached out and touched them, they'd fall apart and float to the broken wood beneath the window.

Morris leaned over and kissed me. I rubbed my hand through his dark, tousled hair as I returned his kiss. His gray eyes bore into my chest, flushing my skin with heat as his hands raced over my hips.

"Goddamn, you were incredible today. Who wouldn't stop for someone like you?" he whispered against my mouth as he bunched my slip at my waist.

Someone cleared their throat from the doorway, and I

recognized that sound. My crazy Vernon. I knew they'd both want me, and I welcomed it.

"Come on, Vernon," I said through panting breaths as I waved him over to me.

Vernon stripped off his slacks and shoes on his way toward us and tapped my thigh to move over. He sat on the edge of the bed and lay down. His cock was hard beneath his boxers.

Morris fisted my hair, helped me to my feet, and pushed me forward with his knee. I leaned over and drew Vernon from the fabric of his shorts. He tasted like sweat as I wrapped my mouth around him, but I didn't care.

Morris' hungry hands were on my waist as he spread my legs and pushed himself inside me. The robberies made me wet enough for all four men, but I could only handle two at a time. Two typically paired off these days. Morris and Vernon, crazed and horny. Reaper and Ricky, who fucked to relieve stress.

I liked fucking one at a time best, though. Nothing to focus on but a cock in my pussy.

Vernon fisted my hair, using it to guide the speed and depth that he needed. Morris thrust deep inside me. Vernon was too tall to fuck me like that. Logistics were a bitch. My knees ached from the wooden bedframe grinding against them with the strength behind Morris' thrusts. I moaned, which vibrated Vernon's cock. There was so much groaning and moaning that the room felt electrified.

"God, I love you, sweets. And your pussy," he groaned as he leaned over and bit my shoulder. He pushed all his love through me, and I poured it into Vernon as he sat up and kissed me.

"Sil," he growled as he pulled my hair from the clasp. "I need you. Your mouth isn't enough."

"I know."

None of them liked to come from my mouth. Every so

often, I could get them going enough to spill their load down my throat, but most of the time they waited impatiently to get inside me so they could come where they wanted to the most.

I dropped my head, resting it on Vernon's warm thigh as I stroked him. I moaned and pushed against Morris' cock. His hands climbed my body and grabbed my shoulders. He fucked me hard enough that I worried I wouldn't be able to take Vernon. And I had to take him. He was being so damn patient.

"My girl," Morris whispered in my ear as he slowed his thrusts, leaving himself deep inside me, pulsing. He said that every time he came, and the words were always laced with adoration. I was his.

Morris pulled out of me and drew me up to him for a kiss. "Thank you, sweets." He zipped his pants up and left me with Vernon, who was dripping with excitement. A bead of it slipped from the head of his dick.

"Finally, Sil," he said as he pulled me onto his lap. His lips found mine, his hand lacing through my hair to nestle against the back of my neck. The come from Morris stained Vernon's boxers, but he didn't care. In this particular arrangement, no one could be averse to another man's come inside me or coating their dicks.

"I need your pussy," he whispered as he guided himself inside me.

I gasped at his size. I'd never get used to it. He was so tall, and his dick matched his stature. *Every* time he slipped inside me, I was reminded of it. There was a slick sound as he thrust upward and into me, sending Morris' come sliding down the length of his dick. I rode his cock, enjoying the wet sounds of excitement between us.

I loved feeling used like that.

Vernon kissed me, grinding his pelvis against mine. He reached his hand between us and rubbed my clit, and the sounds between us intensified. I moaned as he brought me closer to my edge. I wanted to come, to add another remnant of pleasure between us all.

"Fuck, I can't hold out," he groaned in frustration. His taut muscles gleamed with sweat, and he stopped my hips mid-motion so he could come inside me. He liked to stop and unleash all his pleasure inside me while my pussy drew his come from him. That was his thing, and weird as it was, it didn't surprise me.

I climbed off him, my legs trembling and weak.

He caught my arm. "Oh no, I'm not done with you."

He threw me down on the bed, and like the crazy fuck he was, he buried his face in my pussy, licking up every bit of come from me. His, Morris', and soon my own. His tongue raced along my skin, and there was no hesitation in his dark eyes as he lapped up the pearls of pleasure dripping from me. Every flick of his tongue tantalized me, electrifying my entire body. He pressed the flesh of his tongue against my sensitive clit in long, patient strokes. I wove my fingers through his thick hair, pulling him closer until his nose was buried in my pussy as well. His growl vibrated against me, ripping through me as he made me come hard against his mouth.

I shouldn't have chosen favorites, but Vernon was right up there. There wasn't an ounce of inhibition in his body, and he made me feel alive. Fucking him was like being fucked by something inhuman, and nothing would derail him from what he wanted. And he wanted me.

But Vernon's reckless behavior came with a price. It always brought trouble to us.

Chapter 3

I stuck my hand out the window of the car and moved it through the wind as we drove further north toward a farm on the outskirts of the state. The drive felt like an eternity. We were going to pick up the moonshine, which was made in illegal stills on some farms around us. The bootleg industry kept calling for us. None of us wanted to create rivals aside from the law itself, but what choice did we have? Clean up? Get married? Have some kids and a picket fucking fence? No. That wasn't the life I wanted, nor did it seem in the cards for me. Maybe one day, but not now.

Even if people could overlook our criminal pasts, no one would accept our lifestyle and our love for one another. We went against what people considered "normal." Normalcy involved marriage to one man who I'd watch work himself to death for pennies, and he would leave me feeling worth that much as well. I was barren. If you didn't have a baby on your hip and an unhappy husband on your side, what did you have?

I had everything, all that I could ever want, and unless I knew we could all be together, I never wanted out of the lifestyle.

Ricky's lips were tight. I still didn't know why he was so tense, so rigid about what we were doing, but I felt the need to comfort him and slow his racing heart. I reached over and grabbed his hand, slick with sweat. I told him we'd be okay. None of the other leggers gave a damn about us because we were small fish and there were much bigger ones to fry. If we laid low and did our job, we had nothing to worry about.

Reaper pulled onto the long dirt road leading up to a farm. Chickens scratched and pecked at the grass to either side of the car. We drove until the farmhouse came into view. Goats and cows called to us as we pulled up to the front of the home and piled out of the car. I squatted to pet a lanky tabby cat who brushed his body against my legs.

"Come on, sweets," Morris said as he ushered me away from the cat, who began to howl in protest.

Morris knocked on the old wooden door. A family man answered.

"Can I help you, boys?" the man asked.

"Wichita?" Morris asked. That was our code word, and it brought a question to the front of my mind. Was that where Morris came from? If it was, he wouldn't confirm it.

The farmer nodded and closed the door behind him as he stepped onto the porch.

"Do you have all the crates?" Morris asked.

The farmer tightened his lips. "All but three."

Vernon pushed to the head of the group and squared off in front of the burly farmer. Reaper grabbed his shoulder and held him back.

"Calm the hell down, Vernon." Reaper turned toward the farmer. "Why the short?"

"Leak in the still." The farmer walked to the barn and opened the door. He kicked at the rust-eaten still and spit chew onto the ground as he moved a sheet from a stack in the corner, revealing bottles and bottles of moonshine. He reached in and handed Reaper a bottle of the clear liquid. Reaper passed it to Vernon to test it.

Vernon removed the jar's lid and took a giant swig. He choked down the burning liquid. "God, that's good," Vernon groaned, despite the twist in his face at the taste.

"Get this shit loaded up," Reaper said, gesturing to the car.

We filled the car with crates of moonshine and covered it with the sheet from the barn. The glass containers rattled as we stacked them, one on top of another.

Ricky's posture remained tense throughout the entire ordeal. I knew it had to do with bootlegging, but I didn't know the exact details. I felt guilty that he was getting involved with something that was clearly so damn difficult for him.

With the car loaded up, we climbed inside and made our way toward the speakeasy.

WE ARRIVED JUST as a light rain began to fall. It would pass by the time we finished our business. We pulled the car up to the alley so we could enter through the side entrance with our goods without being spotted by the nosy law.

The leader of that particular speakeasy was nothing special. His name was Strawdog, and he had at least twenty years on all of us. He led a small-time gang, a bit bigger than ours. They wanted underground bars, but we just wanted to move products and money. We were in it for ourselves and not one person more. Instead of trying to get rich, we just wanted to survive. Each robbery or sale of booze got us enough money until the next opportunity presented itself. We didn't take more than we needed, and we never got greedy. Reaper always said that was how the others got caught. Greed. A gangster's true nemesis.

"Where's one of the bottles?" came a deep voice from beside us. The man rattled the crate, and the glass clinked with a more audible *clang* because of the missing bottle.

Vernon stumbled a step and tried to focus his eyes. He reached into his pocket, pulled out the nearly empty jar, and tossed it to the man beside the leader. His right hand. If anyone was the right hand of Reaper, it had to be Vernon. He belched as Strawdog narrowed his eyes.

"Just testing the product. It's good."

The right-hand man ironically called himself Whiskey. A cigarette dangled from his thin lips. He took a spoon from his pocket and poured some of the moonshine into it. He lit it with a pack of matches and held the flaming spoon to his cigarette, lighting it. The flame burned a warm blue. It passed the test.

"Told . . . ya," Vernon stammered. To get a guy as big as Vernon drunk, it must have been good shit.

"Wait, they're three cases short," Whiskey said as he dramatically counted the crates. "Where's the rest?"

"Our contact had a leak in their still. He'll make up for it in the next batch. It's no big deal," Morris said in an even tone.

"It's a big fucking deal when we have demand but not enough supply. Do ya understand what I'm saying?"

None of us did, nor did we fucking care. It was his problem. If we wanted to be in that line of work, we would have been. Was he implying he'd kill us? The farmer? Fuck if I knew.

Reaper drew his jacket back at Strawdog's threatening tone, exposing the revolver tucked inside his shoulder holster. The others did the same. Strawdog and Whiskey flexed back with their pistols. Sweat dripped down Ricky's temple, his muscles so rigid it made his hand shake.

"Keep your hands off the product next time, fucking greaseball," Whiskey grumbled as he holstered his gun.

"Better watch yourself," Vernon snarled. The vein on his forehead pulsed, and his face burned red with anger . . . and alcohol.

"What are you gonna do about it?" Strawdog said with a laugh. He took a step toward Vernon.

Knowing exactly what Vernon would do about it, everyone leapt in front of him. It took all four of us to hold him back, even when he was soused as shit.

Reaper whipped his head around to face Strawdog. "I fuckin' wouldn't if I were you."

Vernon was crazy, and we knew what he'd do if we let him get at Strawdog or Whiskey. He was frying fish, and none of us were hungry. We wanted no trouble—well, trouble we didn't cause—and this was *not* how you stayed out of the fray.

"Fuck you," Vernon hissed as we ushered him back to the car. "Fucking prick." He put his arms up and pushed us away from him. "I'm fine. Get off me."

"You don't look fine," Morris said.

"I'm *fine*!"

We all knew he wasn't, but we let it go.

On the drive home, I sat on Vernon's lap, brushing my hand through his hair. His fingers thrummed against my thigh.

"How many times do I have to say it?" he said. "I'm hardly fucking Italian."

"You look Italian, that's all," I said with a smirk. "Tall . . . dark . . ." I stopped myself with a kiss on his forehead. "A handsome son of a bitch."

"When you put it like that." He let a smile creep across his face for a moment before drawing me into his chest. He smelled like alcohol with a hint of corn. "I want you," he whispered against my ear, his warm breath blowing my hair from my neck. "I want you so goddamn bad."

Looking up at me with intense, slightly crazy eyes, he started to unbuckle his belt. I looked around at the others. Ricky flashed me a smile and a nod. Morris tapped Reaper's thigh and they both looked at me through the rear-view mirror.

"It's a long drive home, doll," Reaper said with a low tone and a smile on his face.

Fuck it. I lifted my skirt as Vernon worked down the button of his slacks. He pushed them down as far as he could in the cramped backseat of the car. I straddled his waist and lowered myself onto the heat of his cock, taking its perfection inside me. He groaned into the crook of my neck. My motions were limited, but it didn't matter. Burying him inside me was fucking incredible.

His massive hands gripped my hips and helped move me with each thrust as I grinded against him. I moaned into the salty skin of his neck and looked over at Ricky, who had pulled himself out and was stroking his dick. It made me weak. I wanted Reaper to pull over right then so I could have more space to take them, but we couldn't. We had to keep driving.

Soft moans left Ricky's lips, and the heated exhales between us all began to fog the back windows. Vernon wrapped a powerful arm around my waist. He was going to stop thrusting, ready to come for me, but I didn't want that. Not yet. I pulled off his lap, and a frustrated groan escaped his throat.

I leaned over Ricky's lap and took him into my mouth. Vernon pushed up the fabric of my dress and buried his face between my legs, licking up the wetness he caused. Ricky groaned as I moved my mouth with the gentle pulse of his hips. My moans vibrated his dick. Ricky had already worked himself up, and by the twitch of his balls, I knew he was close.

I pulled away, flashing my eyes up at him as I stroked him. "Will you come for me, angel?"

Ricky pulled me in for a kiss, biting my lower lip. I tried to pull away to put my mouth on him, but he held my face. I continued to stroke him. Groans slipped over his tongue as he bit my lip harder. He released me but captured my mouth with his again as his warm beads of pleasure spilled down my hand. I could only hold my hand there while it dripped down my pale skin as Vernon dragged me to the edge of my orgasm and pushed me off it. I came hard, crying out against Ricky's chest.

"Now get your ass back over here." Vernon yanked me onto his lap. With his mouth and chin slick with my come, he selfishly fucked me until he finished. "I fucking love you, Sil," he groaned against my mouth as he came.

I sighed, taking a moment to enjoy the stillness around us. It was the calm before the storm. I could feel it in the air.

Chapter 4

The crowd around us cheered. Men grappled and pounded at each other with balled fists, creating a symphony of nauseating and relentless sounds. Reaper sat beside me, elbows on his thighs, money fanning between his splayed legs. I bit my nails. I didn't know how they stayed so calm. Morris watched the fight with an intense gaze, the heel of his foot tapping the sticky concrete floor beneath the wooden chair. Ricky reclined his head with his fedora over his eyes, somehow napping through the sounds of hollering and crunching bones.

We were in an abandoned building, which was a big upgrade from the streets. The windows were cracked and painted black to hide the nature of what lived inside. Humans fighting like animals.

I turned my attention back to the audience. Money changed hands. The men in the ring fought for money. Others bet on them, and some lost great amounts to an unlucky choice. Some men wore suits like my boys, while others covered their frames with raggy jackets and wool pants. The rich and the poor mingled together and feasted on bloodlust at the same table.

Reaper put a large sum of money on Vernon. I mean, who wouldn't? But I hated watching them fight. It was barbaric and cruel, and the referees weren't reffing for shit. They made calls when they shouldn't and didn't make them when they should.

Vernon came out from the shadows in a pair of aged slacks painted with blood from prior fights. Some was his, but most of the stains were from others. His suspenders stretched over the broad muscles of his bare shoulders and chest. Rumor had it his pants slipped down once during a fight, which made him lose. He vowed to never let it happen again. Others said he wore them for luck. Either way, he rarely needed luck. Shirtless, bloodied pants, goddamn suspenders—he looked insane.

His competitor? An equal-size man. He wore a loose evening shirt, half-unbuttoned, and wool pants cut at the thighs.

At that place, there were no rounds. They fought until someone couldn't anymore. They paid out the earnings as men lay mortally wounded and dying in the center of the ring. Celebratory shouting often erupted as the losing contender took his final breath.

A well-dressed man rang a bell to signal the start of the fight, and Vernon and the man grappled the moment the shrill sound filled the air. Vernon's muscles flexed as he threw hooks at the man's head, not a hint of hesitation in his swing. Every time the other man made contact, his fists slid across Vernon's skin, which was why he fought shirtless. It was hard to get a solid hit or grasp on him.

It was incredible to see Vernon's ripped physique in the most primal and barbaric contact sport imaginable. Blood flew around them, splattering onto his chest and the ring's floor like paint on a canvas. The crimson liquid dripped in fat lines as the other man grew tired. He gripped Vernon, trying to keep on his feet. His hand slipped beneath the strap of his suspenders and ripped the fabric.

Oh no, I thought with a quick breath.

That gesture infuriated Vernon. He released an otherworldly scream and pushed the man, took a step back, and speared him with his body. He kept him pinned as he ripped the torn strap that was still attached to his pants and wrapped the goddamn thing around the man's neck. Through bubbled, swollen eyes and a bloody nose, the man threw his hands up to try to catch the strap.

I wrapped my hand over my mouth and watched Vernon strangle the life out of this poor sap just for ripping his fucking suspenders. I looked at the ref, who wasn't paying a lick of attention. Or he just didn't give a shit.

Vernon's face turned the color of beet juice. No one did anything to stop what was happening. The raucous cheers drowned out the gagging and choking in the middle of the room. I couldn't take it, so I ran to the center of the makeshift ring and grabbed Vernon's shoulder. He drove his arm back and knocked me on my ass.

"Vernon, stop!" I screamed.

He didn't let go at first, but as if coming back from a trance, he released the two sides of the strap, clambered off the man, and hocked a wad of spit at the ground beside him.

"Fucking wop!" Vernon called to the gasping man on the ground who'd done nothing more than draw the wrong contender's card.

Vernon looked back at me, his expression becoming human again. His eyes softened with concern. "Shit, Sil!" He ran to me and leaned down to help me to my feet. When he saw the anger twisting my features and reddening my pale cheeks, he tried to explain. "I didn't know you were behind me. What're you doing? That was real stupid."

"I didn't want you to kill him," I said with a groan as I grabbed his hand. The others caught up to us as I got to my feet.

Reaper looked down at me. A red rage flushed his cheeks. "Car!" Reaper pointed toward the rickety metal doors.

I bit my lip and defiantly folded my arms across my chest.

"Go!"

Being petulant would get me nowhere, so I ran to the car as they collected their winnings. I leaned against the hot metal and smoked a cigarette while I waited. I spotted Whiskey and Strawdog near the building. My cheeks flushed.

My men poured out of the warehouse and came toward me. Vernon's face and hands were bloodied, but no worse for wear. Morris and Ricky were quiet, and Reaper was counting his money. I tipped my head toward the wall of the building where Whiskey and Strawdog kept their backs pressed against the concrete.

Reaper and Vernon tensed. Morris tugged me into him. The duo pushed off the wall and made their way to us.

"Boys," Strawdog said as he stopped with some distance between us and them.

"Did I hear you calling that man a wop in there?" Whiskey asked.

"Fuck you," Vernon said between clenched teeth.

"Pot, meet kettle," Whiskey said through a laugh that changed the air around us.

I noticed the tension in Vernon's body before the others, and I reached for his arm. He yanked it out of my reach, but Reaper and Morris caught him before he could make a move.

"You sure like to shit talk when you know my men will hold me back," Vernon snarled. "One of these days, they ain't gonna be there, and I'm gonna make it hurt to fucking breathe, let alone crack jokes."

"As hot tempered as he is dumb," Whiskey quipped.

Vernon stepped back and seemed to relax. I let out a breath, my relief coming too soon as he tried to spear his way through Reaper and the others. He was desperate to get his hands on Whiskey. He wanted to wear his blood.

"Stop, Vernon!" Reaper commanded as he strained against Vernon's body. He turned his face toward Strawdog. "What the hell do you want, anyway?"

"The short," Strawdog said. He tossed his cigarette on the ground and squelched it with his shoe.

Reaper scoffed. "I told you, when the next batch is done, we'll make up the difference."

Strawdog set his jaw. "See, that's not going to work for us."

Reaper took a step toward them. "It's gonna have to."

"Or you can just hand us some of those winnings," Whiskey said.

Reaper smirked at him as he pocketed the money. "You'll get the extra booze in the next batch."

A man called out to Whiskey and Strawdog, and they looked back and gave him a lazy nod before returning their attention to Reaper. "This isn't over," Strawdog said with a sneer as he and Whiskey walked toward the waiting car.

Reaper tipped his hat and got into the driver's seat.

"You could have just paid them," Morris said.

Reaper scoffed. "Nah, that's not how this is going to work."

We stayed silent on the car ride back to our hideout. It should have been filled with the excitement of the win, but the air was too heavy with the scent of blood and frustration. Reaper kept his hands tight on the wheel. Vernon babied his right knuckle. Dried blood caked his chin from a cut on his lip. He kept his gaze on the floor in front of him.

"Can someone tell me what's the matter with you all?" I screamed, sick of the tension between me and all of them. "It was just a little short with—"

"That's not it," Ricky whispered. "You shouldn't get involved with fights."

Everyone else stayed quiet, showing me that pulling Vernon away after the fight had pissed them all off. What the fuck ever. What was I supposed to do? Let Vernon kill the man?

When we got into the house, Vernon wrapped his arm around me and kissed my forehead. "I'm sorry I pushed you." Reaper put a rough grasp on my arm, and Vernon stared him down. "Don't you lay a hand on her, Reaper. She didn't know no better."

"I ain't going to hurt her," Reaper said, ripping me from his grasp. He dragged me to the bedroom and pinned me against the wall.

My nostrils flared and my cheeks puffed as I stared into his dark eyes. "What?" I snapped at him.

"We fuckin' bet that Vernon would rage out and kill a man. We'd have gotten twice the money if you hadn't acted like such a *woman* and interfered."

Fuck you. I was lost for words. Actually, I had plenty of words I *wanted* to say. "You told Vernon to do that to that man?"

"Of course not. It's Vernon, for Christ's sake. There's a fifty-fifty chance he'd end up mad enough to kill."

"How the fuck was I supposed to know you made some bet?"

"Watch your mouth, doll."

"Or what?" I puffed out my chest.

Reaper smiled and picked me up, tossing me over his shoulder. I punched at his back, which did absolutely jack shit against his muscles. He carried me to the living room and set me down on the couch.

"I ain't going to do shit to you," he said as he grazed my cheek with his hand. Reaper had never laid his hands on me. Not even over money. He leaned down and kissed me. "I love you, even though you cost us a hell of a lot of money."

"I can't believe you called that man a wop," Ricky said, breaking the tension with a laugh. "You're a goddamn wop, Vernon."

Vernon snapped his gaze to Ricky. "I'm not even a quarter Italian, you fucking mick."

Ricky tightened his lips. "I'm hardly Irish."

"You're both mutts. Quit it," Morris said.

"We could figure it out, Ricky." Vernon cracked his bloody knuckles.

Ricky stood up, cracked his neck, and rushed toward Vernon. His spidery movements caught Vernon off guard. Vernon was stronger, but he'd have to catch Ricky first. Ricky's laughter filled the room as they playfully grappled and wrestled on the ground. Ricky grabbed my arm and pulled me down with them, and I squealed as I tried to avoid Vernon's bloody hands.

"Stop it!" I said through laughter while pawing at their hands.

The boys ended their mock scuffle and sat back, and I rested my head in Ricky's lap, catching my breath. Vernon leaned over me, his thighs on either side of my body, and kissed me as Ricky rubbed his hand through my hair.

There was so much love in that goddamn room. There had to be. Life was too short for us to be anything but in love.

Chapter 5

Ricky crawled into bed with me, and I welcomed him beneath the sheet. The night was much too warm for anything more. The stale, hot air sent prickles of sweat rising over my skin. He put his fedora on the bedside table and turned onto his back. He looked up at the aging ceiling above our heads. His lips were drawn tight, the pulse in his cheeks showcasing his frustration.

"Angel, how did you even get into this lifestyle?" I asked as I rolled onto my side and caught his gaze.

He gave me a side smirk and tucked his arm beneath my head. "My brother," he said with a bite of his lip. I knew in my heart that Ricky hadn't ended up in this life by choice. He wasn't cut out for it.

"You never told me what happened to him."

He cleared his throat. "You know how much I hate bootlegging? It's because he was taken out by goddamn lawmen at a suspected speakeasy. There was so much fucking money in illegal booze, he couldn't resist. That's why I don't drink the stuff. Nothing but pain and death comes from it. Before he died, we only had each other, and had the boys not kept me around, I'd have probably added a bullet hole to my body."

I swallowed hard, my lips pursed. The thought of Ricky shooting himself broke my heart. He didn't even want to pull the trigger on men who deserved it, yet he'd considered doing it to the one who deserved it the least. I shuddered at the thought of his blond hair caked with deep crimson. It made me sick, and ain't nothing made me feel that way.

"Don't look at me like that, love. I have you, and come hell or high water, nothing would keep me from you. I know I ain't like the rest, but I'd take one in the chest to protect you and wait for you behind the gates of hell. I fucking love you." He pulled me to his mouth and kissed me. His touch made me shiver. "Besides, you didn't end up here in the most conventional way, either." He smirked against my mouth.

He was right. I wasn't a conventional member of that gang. I was collateral. I was a walking liability that should have been killed, but feelings got in the way of that when Reaper looked down his barrel at me, ready to do the deed he needed to do. I don't know if it was because I could outdrink them or beat them in cards or because I refused to plead for my life, but he couldn't pull the trigger. He'd given me the option to leave—walk the hell outta there and go back to my boring fucking life—and what did I do? I stayed. When he spared me, Reaper only asked that I didn't make him regret it. I never did.

I smirked at the memory. Facing death himself and surviving. Facing death and making love to him later that night. *Fuck*. Not only had I felt more loved than I ever had in my life, they laid off my mama. She never had to worry about that debt again. Not from my boys, at least.

I grew with them in ways I never thought possible. In ways I shouldn't have. I used to be afraid of killing, and it kept me up at night on more than one occasion, but the more I saw men fall, the less it bothered me. Pretty soon, I only hesitated for half a heartbeat before I pulled the trigger.

"I love you, angel," I whispered into the darkness. "I wouldn't let you take a bullet for me, so kiss that idea goodbye. When it's my time, it's my time. I had a fantastic fucking run."

Ricky's hand slid down my side. Sometimes I wondered if Ricky wanted out of this life. Maybe he even wanted me to go with him. He had to know I wouldn't leave the others. Not in this lifetime. Maybe not even the next. We were all stuck together.

Reaper came into the room, his shirt unbuttoned and spreading open as he walked. He stopped at the side of the bed and rubbed a hand through my hair. "Beat it." He gestured to Ricky, pointing him toward the door with a jerk of his chin.

Disappointment sprang across Ricky's face, but no one dared to defy Reaper. He slid out of bed and tugged at the front of his boxers in uncomfortable frustration before leaving us together.

"Doll . . ." he groaned as he leaned down and kissed me. Reaper looked nothing like the skeletal imagery you'd imagine beneath the robe of the grim reaper. He was so damn strong. His taut muscles called to me from beneath the loose flaps of his unbuttoned dress shirt. He pulled a cigarette from his shirt pocket and lit it before stripping away the sticky, sweat-stained fabric. Smoke swirled through the stagnant air.

"What do you want?" I asked with a bite of my lip.

His cigarette dangled from an erotic smirk. "I want you to remind me why I spared you." He loved to remind me of that, though he saved me without ever knowing if I'd lay with him willingly or walk out that door and never look back.

I'd get beneath Reaper whenever he asked, not because I had to, but because I wanted to. I was the only person in the goddamn world who could tell him no without coming face to face with a bullet, but that wasn't an issue. I needed him inside me as much as he needed to be inside me. I was allowed to be weak with Reaper. I was tough, but sometimes I grew tired of being so hard. I *let* Reaper control me, not the other way around.

"But what do you want?" I asked again.

He grabbed my arm, pulled me toward the edge of the bed, and rolled me onto my belly. With a strong, confident grip, he raised my hips. I bit my lip and whimpered when he landed a slap on my ass. There was no avoiding the stinging pain that followed.

"I want your ass," he groaned, rubbing a finger along the reddening skin. Reaper was the only one who liked to fuck my ass, but I'd let Reaper do anything to me, except kill me. But if the situation called for it, I'd want it to be his finger on the trigger.

The buckle of his belt clanged as he unfastened it. The sound of leather being ripped from the loops of his pants made my heart thrum in my chest. Instead of hitting me with it—which I expected—he let it fall to the ground with a *thud*. He unbuttoned his pants, pulled himself from his boxers, and rubbed his warm cock against my ass, leaving lines of his excitement on me as he dripped with anticipation. He spit in his hand, and my racing heart clogged my ears with its beat. I awaited the pleasurable pain as he rubbed the spit on his dick before pushing inside me. When a whimper slipped from my parted lips, he waited before pushing further.

"Reaper," I groaned, fighting the twitch in my muscles to reach back and push against him.

"You okay, doll?" he asked as he spit on his hand again.

I nodded, my teeth clenched. I was fine once he was in, but getting him there was rough. He inched himself further inside me, ignoring my whimpers because he knew if he didn't, it would take too fucking long to get there. Like jumping into a goddamn lake and getting the initial rush of freezing temperature behind you. He groaned as he buried himself to the hilt inside me, and I dropped my chest to the mattress.

His thrusts weren't gentle when he was in my pussy, but in my ass, he was a fucking gentleman. He leaned over and grinded his hips deeper into me. I reached down and rubbed myself, finding all the pleasure I could. I almost wished for a cock in my pussy. I hadn't taken them together like that before.

"Reaper? Can you get Ricky?" I finally gathered the courage to ask.

He lifted my chest to get a look at me, his eyebrow lifted. "What are you thinking of doing?"

"I want you both."

"Is that what you really want?" He brushed my hair away from my wet cheeks and pulled out of me. After tucking himself into his boxers, he disappeared, leaving me feeling so goddamn empty. I swirled with anticipation.

What was I thinking? Did I really want to open myself up to two men at once? It was one thing to lean over and let one use my mouth while the other used my pussy, but what I suggested was something very different.

Reaper did what I asked, bringing a smiling Ricky back to me. He also had a glass jar in his hand. He popped it open, smelled it, and ran his fingers through the pale-yellow liquid. He put a drop on his tongue.

"Olive oil," he said with a smile. "If we're doing what you're thinking about, I need it. Well, you need it."

I stood and let Ricky strip before lying on the bed where I had been sitting. I climbed over him, straddling his waist and kissing him.

"Are you sure, love?" Ricky asked as he drew his mouth from mine.

I smiled at him. I was so goddamn sure. We both dripped with excitement as I guided him inside me.

"Fuck," Ricky groaned, dropping his head back. "You definitely want both of us?" he asked once more.

I bit my lip instead of answering him and leaned my chest forward, arching my back for Reaper and kissing Ricky into silence. Reaper came behind me and dripped the cold oil down my ass. Goosebumps rose on my skin as my body heat warmed it and made it slicker. Reaper stroked himself before pushing into my ass again. I screamed out, not from pain—though there was pain—but from the unbelievably full feeling.

Reaper lost his inhibition that time, thrusting himself deep from the start, as if he wanted to compete with Ricky. Every small thrust from Ricky pulled me down and away from Reaper's heavy hand. There was no competition between those two. They were both incredible. I relinquished myself to the tug and pull of my body as Reaper grabbed my hips, grinding into me.

It was unexplainable.

"You guys are going to make me come. Fuck," I moaned, dropping my face to Ricky's. He kissed me, wrapping a hand around my neck and keeping me from pulling away from him.

"Do you feel fuckin' full, doll?" Reaper asked, digging his fingers into the flesh of my ass.

"You have no idea," I whispered, as I pulled my face from the curve of Ricky's neck. Sweat dripped down my chest and dropped onto Ricky's bare stomach. The weight of Reaper's body as he drove his hips into me rubbed my clit against Ricky's pelvis.

"Come, love," Ricky whispered into my ear.

I did. I exploded with an orgasm that made me lose track of time. Of what goddamn day it was. It made me forget everything that didn't involve the gravelly groan of Reaper behind me and the soft moans of Ricky beneath me. When they rode my spasms, they groaned in near unison. It was a full body experience I wouldn't forget anytime soon.

They filled me up as they came, and I was somewhere closer to heaven than hell at that moment. Not even the devil could pull me back down when I was locked in the embraces of an angel and death himself.

Chapter 6

Morris tugged me into him on the couch. His fingers swirled around the rim of a mason jar filled with moonshine. He stroked my hair with a tense look.

"What's wrong?" I asked.

He leaned in and kissed my forehead. "Nothing, sweets. Just got things on my mind."

I grabbed his chin and brought my lips to his. "Tell me."

"I just don't trust Strawdog's gang. I don't like working with them. Strawdog has a look in his eye that I recognize, and I don't like it."

"Recognize from your past?" I pried, hoping to get more of his history.

"I know what you're doing, sweets." He smirked and kissed me. "How many times have I told you to stop poking your pretty nose into my past?" He didn't say it in a mean way.

"But..."

Morris cut off my questions by pulling me onto his lap and letting his tongue explore mine. He leaned back and looked into my eyes. "The only way to keep you from asking questions is by playing around with you, huh?"

"No," I said with a smile.

"I know you want to know things about me. I know that. But who I am now is not who I used to be. That person is dead, and you don't need the history of a dead man." He looked up at me. "You're my girl," he whispered as he wrapped my hair in his fist. "That's all that matters."

"I love you," I whispered as I dropped my head into his neck. "I just want to know *who* you are."

There was nothing Morris could say that would make me think of him in a different way or see him as anyone else but the sweet, confident man beneath me. Even so, he stayed tight-lipped about who he used to be.

"Stop prying." Reaper's booming voice broke through our playful haze. I met his gaze. "I've known Morris for almost a decade, and he's been Morris for that long at least."

"Don't worry your pretty head about me, sweets." Morris turned to look at Reaper. "Vernon's been gone a long time for just a simple drop. Think he's okay?"

Reaper scoffed. "I'm sure he's fine. A monkey with a backpack could have settled that debt."

The moment the door opened, I knew something was wrong. Everything was wrong. My breaths hitched when the tone in the room shifted as Morris guided me off his lap, letting his hand linger on my hip before I dropped beside him. An ominous heaviness came in with Vernon, and everyone's eyes were glued to him. His lips were tight. Blood covered his white dress shirt. More crimson marred the skin of his neck and arms. Another blotch of blood streaked his cheek, as if he'd wiped the back of his hand over his sweaty skin.

"Vernon . . ." Reaper took a step toward him.

Ricky walked into the room, his mouth agape at the horrific sight.

"I fucked up," Vernon said with a sigh.

"What'd you do?" Morris rose to his feet.

Vernon scoffed. "Whiskey."

My mouth dropped open. That wasn't good. If he'd done what I thought he'd done, we would all be fucked. That was *not* how to get in, do the job, and get out. This was the opposite of laying low.

Oh, Vernon.

"What'd you do?" Reaper pressed.

When Vernon didn't respond, Reaper pushed him against the door frame, drew his arm back, and punched him in the jaw. The hit did nothing to sway Vernon. He shook his head and reached up to touch his cheek. Reaper pushed him further into the wall.

"This ain't just about you, Vernon! What the fuck did you do? Did you fuckin' kill him?"

Vernon shook his head. "Nah, I just messed him up a bit. That's all."

"You know what happens when you mess people up," Morris said. "They end up dead."

Vernon rolled his sleeves up, hiding some of the blood. "He's not gonna die. Let it go."

"You go and put a target on our backs, and I'm supposed to just let it go?" Reaper snarled. "Life ain't about you anymore, Vernon. You don't run alone any longer. You have a family now!"

"You think I don't know that?"

"Get out of my fuckin' sight." Reaper gestured away from him.

Vernon stared for a moment, his eyes narrowing before he thought better of arguing. He disappeared down the hall to shower.

"Now what?" Ricky asked as he took steps toward Reaper.

"I told you he was gone too long. He shouldn't have been anywhere near their gang," Morris said as he wrapped a protective arm around my waist. "He doesn't realize he's fucked up until after he's done the fucking up." Morris sighed. "I don't like them. I was just telling her I don't trust them, and Vernon went and stirred up more trouble."

"I know, Morris," Reaper snapped.

"Do you, though? Because he's always stepping out without your graces."

Reaper narrowed his eyes at Morris. "The thing about Vernon, Morris, is that he's not fuckin' sane enough to listen to my graces. Vernon is Vernon, and now we have to clean up his mess like we always do. It is what it is. There's no us without Vernon. When we started this gang, I went into it knowing he was a loose cannon."

"It's different now, Reaper. We have her now." Morris rubbed his hand down my side.

Reaper groaned. "Yeah, and I would give my life to protect her." He turned to Ricky. "Load up the guns. We're going first thing in the morning to try to do some goddamn damage control. Load 'em up, but hopefully we don't need 'em."

"When are we going?" I asked.

Reaper turned a harsh gaze toward the bathroom. He spun on his heels and locked his gaze on mine. "*We* aren't going anywhere, Silvia. You ain't going. Not a chance. If something happens to you—" Reaper shook his head. "If something happens to you, I'll kill Vernon myself."

Reaper never called me by my name, and his tone and posture left no room for argument. I sat back and kept my mouth shut. The way he threatened Vernon made me sure he'd do it. He'd never forgive Vernon if something happened to me.

Chapter 7

The boys had all gone to the speakeasy. They left Vernon behind with me, which was wise. If they planned to smooth it all out, they didn't need his bruised face reminding them of where the trouble came from.

"What the hell were you thinking?" I asked.

"Nothing. I wasn't thinking of shit. That's the problem."

There was a creak on the rickety front porch. Vernon perked up, grabbing his 1911 and racking it.

"It's nothing, Vernon. Relax."

"It's never nothing," Vernon said as he sat taller.

Wood snapped and a deafening crash sounded as the door was kicked in. Vernon stood and placed his body between me and Strawdog, Whiskey, and two others I barely recognized. Whiskey's face was a deep shade of pinkish-purple, and his arm was in a sling.

Vernon drew his pistol. We were grossly outgunned and outnumbered.

"What the fuck do you want?" Vernon snarled, blocking me with his body.

"You broke my friend here," Strawdog said, gesturing

toward Whiskey. "And now we gotta break something of yours."

"Is it a fight you want, 'cause I can give you a fight," Vernon quipped.

"We aren't here for you."

Strawdog smirked before drawing his pistol and shooting. Vernon pulled the trigger, but not before a bullet hit his right arm, sending his shot into the floorboards between the men. I screamed as blood splattered against the wall beside us.

Vernon didn't crumble like they expected, but his blood-soaked arm dropped limp at his side. He held his hand over the wound, his cheeks pulsing with anger and pain. His eyes were as crazed as I'd ever seen them, and his right hand trembled as he tried to gather the strength to raise his pistol. When he looked down, my eyes followed his gaze. The slide was out of battery. A double feed jammed his damn gun.

He reached across and grabbed the jammed pistol in his left hand and tucked it down the back of his pants. "You're going to be goddamn sorry," Vernon said through clenched teeth. "If you lay a hand on her, so help me god, I'll make you wish your mother's mother wasn't fucking born."

Strawdog laughed. "I don't think you're in a position to negotiate."

One of the men behind Whiskey ran for Vernon. Even with an injured arm, he took the man into a grapple. He landed punches, his face twisted in pain. His body ran solely on adrenaline. Blood splatter dripped in a path along the floor, and the other unfamiliar man joined in. Heat welled behind my eyes, and I worried that this was it. I couldn't even call out as Strawdog side stepped the clashing flesh and came toward me.

Just as I gathered my faculties and went for the sawed-off shotgun, he grabbed me so hard I thought he might break my damn arm. I turned my attention back to the fight, and my heart shattered as the men overcame Vernon. Every time he went for his gun, they hit him with one of theirs. They knew they couldn't take him down if he wasn't injured. When he finally went to his knees, Whiskey sent a cheap shot to his face.

"You guys feel real big taking on someone three to fucking one?" I scoffed. "Pathetic."

"Mouthy one, aren't we?" Strawdog said as he ran a hand over my cheek. The flash of anger from my eyes reflected in his irises.

"If I could reach a gun, I'd make sure your own mama wouldn't recognize your face," I snarled.

"God, there's not enough women like you. Are you his?" Strawdog gestured toward Vernon.

"I'm all of theirs."

"Oh?" Strawdog lifted his eyebrow. "They all fuck you?"

I tightened my lips. That eyebrow lifted in curiosity, as if a worse idea had just infiltrated his mind. I didn't respond. I'd said too fucking much already.

"You like to take all those men at once?" Strawdog turned toward Whiskey, rubbing his chin. "Did you hear that, Whisk?"

Whiskey grinned, catching on to his meaning. "I mean, if that's what she likes, we can give it to her. Right, boys?"

"Don't you fucking touch her," Vernon said. He tried to clamber to his feet, but the blood coating the floor proved too slippery. He fell to his hands and knees, his chest heaving with pain and anger.

"Oh, we're going to do more than touch her." Strawdog shook me by my arm.

One of the men hit Vernon with the butt of his rifle. "Stay the fuck down!" he shouted as he took the pistol from Vernon's back.

Vernon's jaw clenched so hard that I was sure his teeth would chip in his mouth. He was done for.

We both were.

Strawdog dragged me toward him. I dug my heels in, but he only tugged harder. I writhed against him, losing the sound of Vernon's voice beneath the racing beat of my heart in my ears.

Strawdog bent me over the couch. I fought against him and screamed, but a hand wrapped around my mouth, preventing me from releasing more than a muffled whimper. My nostrils flared above his dirty hand, and I let a tear slip down my cheek. It stained his skin. His hand shoved my slip over my hips. His touch reminded me of the man in the alleyway, and my heart galloped against the wall of my chest. It would have leapt from my throat had his hand not been over my mouth.

"You just fucking wait," Vernon snarled. "Think before you touch her, because you better kill me if you do."

Strawdog laughed as he unbuttoned his slacks. He pulled his cock from the slit of his pants and pushed himself inside me. I screamed through his hand, trying to pull away from him. Sweat covered my scalp, fear dripping from every pore.

"Goddamn," Strawdog groaned. "Now I know why you all keep her around."

The moment Strawdog forced himself inside me, Vernon abandoned his pain and tried to get to me. They butt stroked him in the head with their rifles, knocking him unconscious.

I was alone with these monsters.

They had no idea what a real monster was, though. Not yet.

My stomach twisted with every quick pulse of his hips into me. He brushed my hair over my shoulder as he bottomed out inside me. He laughed, motioning to Whiskey to join him before he released his hand from my mouth and circled me like a vulture. He brought his limp cock to my face, rubbing it along my lips. The salty taste as he violated my mouth made me writhe. I lunged for him, but Whiskey grabbed my shoulders and tugged me back, pressing me against his lap.

I looked up at Strawdog with hate-filled eyes. "I will rip your fucking dick off, mark my words."

"I very much doubt that, little girl," he said in a mocking tone as he squatted down and brought his face closer to mine. He looked as if he wanted to kiss me where his disgusting cock had touched my mouth. Instead, he patted me on the head, which was maddening.

Whiskey unbuttoned his pants and pushed himself inside me. The slick sound echoed in the room. I'd once been fond of that sound. It represented pleasure and safety when one of my men slipped inside me, chasing the remnants of the other. Now it was a deafening, audible reminder of my torment and degradation.

Whiskey offered sloppy and disinterested thrusts, as if it hurt him to do it. He wasn't going to miss the opportunity to fuck something Vernon loved, though. No way.

I closed my eyes and tried to stop the tears from falling. I didn't want to show them an ounce of weakness. They'd get off on it.

Fuck them.

Whiskey continued slamming into me with uneven thrusts until he pulled out and came on my ass. I gagged at the feeling of his warm come on my skin, somehow worse than inside me, but I couldn't ignore it as it burned through my flesh.

"You don't find molls like her. Fucking tough as steel, I'll give her that." Whiskey turned me around and raised my face to his. "You're something special."

I spit at him, and the thick glob landed on his mouth. He punched me in the face, his bony knuckle sliding along my cheek. The pain blinded me, but aside from the reflexive scream when he struck me, I refused to acknowledge the hit.

"Get on her, Reese, and make it fucking quick. We want to be gone when they get back."

One of the two remaining men came up behind me, but he had a hard time controlling me as I tried to scramble away. Strawdog drew his pistol and put it against my temple. I took a deflated breath and dropped my chest to the arm of the couch once more, his gun forcing my obedience.

The man undid his slacks behind me, but he couldn't get hard, as if the act were too cruel for someone like him. He rubbed his limp dick against me. "Fuck," he mumbled. He slapped it against the wet heat of my pussy and growled. When that didn't work, he smacked my ass so hard that it pushed me and the couch forward. "Fucking cunt," he snarled. It wasn't my fault he was a limp-dicked son of a bitch.

The final man pushed him out of the way. "Move over and let a real man show you how to fuck." He pushed my legs apart with his knee. I just wanted to get it over with at that point. Just hurry the fuck up so I could get the retribution I craved.

Retribution, a four-syllable word. The number of men they wanted me to take. The number of cowards me and my men would hunt down.

The man pushed inside me with his tiny dick, and I dropped my face against the back of the couch, smearing my lipstick on the light fabric. His thrusts were rhythmic but shallow, as if he were a goddamn virgin trying to overcompensate. It was pathetic. If you're going to do it, do it fucking right. Make it fucking worth it, because it better be worth your life.

Vernon made a noise from the ground. I looked back at him. The crazed glare in his eyes was gone, replaced by something so much worse. Something that deadened his irises before my very eyes. Seeing him so weak and hurt shattered my heart. My emotional pain numbed the feeling of the clumsy piece of shit behind me, his thrusts ragged as he came inside me. I could only see the twist of pain on Vernon's bleeding face as the men released me and I crumpled to the floor.

"Good girl," Strawdog whispered as he rubbed my bruised cheek. "I hope this isn't the last time I see you."

It fucking wouldn't be. *That* I could promise him.

As soon as they left, I crawled toward Vernon. He gathered what little strength he had and pulled me into him. His arm was still bleeding from the flesh wound where the bullet grazed him. I tore his shirt, balled it up, and held pressure on the wound as I dropped my head against his. I finally let myself cry, and I released all the pain through my sobs.

"I'm so fucking sorry, Sil. I'm so goddamn sorry." This massive man allowed tears to trail from his eyes as he held me. He was a goddamn gangster, letting himself break down for what was probably the first time in his entire life.

Tires rolled over gravel, and my heart broke once more. They would never look at me the same. They couldn't.

My boys came in, dropping their guns as they crossed the threshold and saw our bloodied, broken, and torn mess.

Ricky gasped. "Oh god." He was the first to reach me. He pulled my hair away from my face, his jaw clenching at the sight of my cheek. As he pulled me away from Vernon and lifted me to my feet, he only saw me. "What happened?"

Morris tried to help Vernon to his feet, but he swatted his hands away. He looked like he might explode. "Give me the fucking keys," Vernon commanded as he spit a gob of blood onto the floor.

Reaper stopped him. "You ain't doing shit tonight. No one's doing a goddamn thing." Reaper pushed Ricky away and took me into his arms. "Please tell me—" He stopped himself and swallowed hard. "Tell me they didn't touch you."

I couldn't hold his stare. It was too intense. Instead, I pleaded with him. "Don't go after Vernon. He tried so—"

"Goddamn it!" He released me rougher than he intended, knocking me back a step. Ricky caught me and helped steady my exhausted body.

Reaper drew his pistol and stepped into Vernon. "That!" He gestured toward me. "That is *your* fucking fault." Reaper cocked the hammer and held it to Vernon's head, his hand trembling with rage. "I should kill you."

"Don't!" I cried out. I tried to run to them, but Morris held me back with an arm around my waist.

I couldn't stand the idea of Vernon being killed over me. I couldn't lose him. Yeah, he pissed them off in the first place, but I was the one who was raped. If I could forgive Vernon, they needed to as well.

"Please don't hurt him!" I screamed. I lost some dignity—well, a lot of dignity—but not enough for Vernon to lose his life. I could recover from a loss of dignity, but I would never recover from watching the man I loved kill another man I loved. I would lose a quarter of what made my heart full.

"Kill me," Vernon said through clenched teeth. "I deserve it."

Reaper's lips tightened and he made a motion to pull the gun away, but Vernon grabbed the barrel, pinning it against his forehead.

"I can't live with what I saw. What I couldn't stop." Vernon pressed the metal further into his flesh. "Please."

Reaper looked back at me, and I shook my head, pleading with him. Nothing would be the same, but we had to figure it the fuck out because that's what we did. That's who we were.

Retribution. Four syllables. Four men to kill.

Chapter 8

Ricky brushed a hand through my hair after I showered, sending water droplets onto my skin. The paths they tracked down my arms left goosebumps in their wake. He couldn't keep his hands off me. He was protecting me from everyone, even the others.

"Love," he said as he touched the bruise on my cheek. "What happened?"

I shook my head. "It's better you don't know."

"I need to know. If you don't want me to tell anyone else, fine, but I have to know what happened to you."

"You won't look at me the same way, angel." I groaned. "Damaged fucking goods."

Ricky's jaw went slack. "Silvia, nothing would ever make me look at you any other way than the way I look at you right now. The way I've always looked at you."

I knew he meant it, down to the tremble of his full lower lip. I also knew he was aware of what happened to me. He hadn't needed to ask, and I couldn't answer. The moment I said it out loud, I admitted it was real. What happened to me would manifest into its own entity, ready to haunt me.

"You know what they did," I whispered, my gaze falling from his. I couldn't even look him in the eye.

"How many?"

"Three of them, but there were four."

Ricky swallowed hard. "Three?" His heart broke. I heard it shatter within his chest. His hands dropped from my body, but not from disgust. He wasn't repulsed by me. He was in shock. We all were. He pulled me closer and met my eyes. "Fuck, Silvia."

"Where's Vernon?"

Ricky's lips tightened. "I don't know why you're so willing to forgive him."

"Because he fought until the very end to protect me."

As if he heard me ask for him, Vernon appeared in the doorway, leaning against the frame with a flinch of pain. His jaw was set, and I knew he had so much racing through his mind. Oh god, he saw so much. He had to watch. I took comfort in knowing he didn't see it all. What he *had* seen was enough.

"Beat it, Ricky," Vernon said, gesturing for him to leave.

"I'm not leaving her with you," Ricky hissed.

"I could beat your ass with my fucked-up arm," Vernon said.

I turned Ricky's face toward mine. "It's fine, angel."

Ricky scoffed. "Are you sure you want to be alone with him?"

"Stop acting like he did anything to me. Vernon would *never* hurt me, and you know that."

"None of this would've happened if it weren't for him."

"I'm fine."

I needed to be alone with Vernon. I had to know what he thought of me. If he still loved me. He had seen the things the others could only conjure in their heads. He saw me being used. Forced. He witnessed the moment I gave in and let it happen.

I didn't just *let* it happen, though. I plotted. I committed their faces to memory. And I would get my revenge.

Ricky bumped into Vernon on his way out of the room.

Vernon stepped forward, keeping a hand where his ribs were most likely broken. His face was cut up and bruised. A bandage wrapped around the bullet wound in his arm. He looked like a mess, but nothing compared to the look in his eyes. It was so unlike Vernon's expression, as if he were someone else entirely. Someone who had shattered the hard shell that made Vernon who he was.

He sat beside me on the bed and drew quick inhales as he pulled me into him, as if fending off the pain. I melted into his touch and dropped my head to his bruised chest.

"Was it all of them?" Vernon asked, his jaw tensing to the point where I heard his teeth grinding together.

"Three of them."

I thought I heard what a heart sounded like when it shattered while I stood beside Ricky, but that sound was nothing compared to that of a heart being ground to dust within Vernon's chest.

"God, Sil." His eyes glossed over, but he fought back the tears by wiping them away with a humorless laugh. "I'll never forgive myself for this. Seeing him . . . his hands . . . your pain . . . " His Adam's apple bobbed beneath the thin skin of his throat.

"Can you even look at me the same?" I got up the balls to ask.

"No, Sil. I can't."

Ricky's shattering heart hurt me. Vernon's crushed heart broke me. But those four words obliterated my heart with a deafening explosion that sent ripples through my blood. It—

"You are so goddamn strong. You're everything I

sometimes forget you could be. The type of woman we ended up with made us keep our guns a little closer at night. A fucking moll, through and through, and ain't no pricks like them gonna change that." He rubbed his chin with his hand. "I fucking love you. And that's why I can't handle this. I can't stand that it happened because of *me*, because of *my* fucking anger. I'd have let them beat me to death if it meant it would have saved you from them. Fuck." He bit his lower lip.

I leaned into him, reveling in the warm breath that slipped past his lips with every exhale. I lifted his chin and kissed him. I loved him so damn much. I straddled his lap, pulling my slip up as I did.

He braced against the pain and grabbed my arms. "No, Sil. I can't."

My eyes glossed over, but instead of holding the tears back as Vernon had, I let them paint my cheeks.

Was it because I was dirty? Because he couldn't imagine being with me after them?

He grabbed my face, flinching as he lifted his right shoulder. "Don't you fucking think what you're thinking."

"What else could it possibly be?"

"I don't want to hurt you."

I scoffed. "Yeah right."

He growled against my chest. "What do you want from me, Sil?"

"I want you to show me that I'm still me. That I'm not broken. That you aren't." I sniffled. "I've never needed you more."

Vernon bit back pain and stood, wrapping my legs around his waist. He pushed me against the wall.

"Don't do this because I begged you. I don't want some pity fuck. If your heart isn't in it, don't bother," I said.

His muscles tensed and flexed as he held me in place. "My heart has never been more in it, Sil. I've wanted to remind you what home feels like since last night, but I'm dealing with my own goddamn shame."

"Give me yours, and you can take mine."

Vernon's lips met mine in a hard and passionate kiss. With every fiber in his broken body screaming for him to stop, he took a step away from the wall so he could pull his boxers down without letting his lips leave mine. He pushed himself into me without hesitation, fear, or judgment. He groaned into my neck, and I dropped my head back. I let myself feel the safety of his arms. I had to show him that my body and mind forgave him.

He blew out a breath. "I gotta stop," he said, his abdomen sucking in from pain. "It's not because I want to. Fuck, I don't want to. I just can't come when I feel like I have a baseball bat grinding into my ribcage. I'll make it up to you, I promise." He kissed me, and I knew I'd let him do exactly that.

WE HAD TO LEAVE. What were we going to do? Wait around like sitting ducks until they came back?

I looked down at the floor as I walked through the living room with my bag. Vernon's dried blood still marked every surface. Reaper tugged me into him when he saw me staring, and I welcomed his touch. He'd been so distant with me since it happened.

"We'll get our revenge, doll. I ain't letting this go." He kissed me, but it wasn't the unstifled display of possession I was used to from him. It was as if he thought his touch would break me, not realizing it would be what glued me back together. There was too much tension between us. All of us.

No one knew how to step around me or take a breath in my presence.

I followed Morris to the car and watched as he put another sack of money beneath the seat. Reaper slid into the driver's seat.

"We gotta get out of here," Morris said. He grabbed my arm and kissed the top of my head before I got in the car. "They're dead, sweets, and we promise to let you get the last slice." He smiled as he slipped a pocketknife into my hand. "It was my pop's." He closed my fist around it. "They didn't change a damn thing about my feelings for you."

I fought back the heat behind my eyes at his words. It was as if he knew how much I needed to hear that right then. I looked back at the house, blinking away my tears. Morris was right. We had to go. There couldn't be any more bloodshed here.

We piled into the car and took off toward the city, keeping our eyes peeled along the way for some place to lay our heads. With a car full of guns and money, a hotel would have been too risky.

We drove until we saw a house with a stack of newspapers on the porch. It was a bit too close to the city for comfort, but we were exhausted, sick of being crammed in the car, and the temperature had crept up until we were all sweating bullets.

Reaper turned and looked at Ricky. "Go knock."

"Why me?"

"Because you look like a little church boy. Go," Reaper said with a laugh. "If someone's home, they won't think nothin' of you."

Ricky got out and jogged up the front steps. He knocked and waited, but no one came to the door. He kicked at the bottom of it to make more noise, and when no lights or movement came from inside, he waved us over.

Reaper pulled the car onto the grass, concealing it behind

a rickety old shed with rusted holes that let light shine inside. We all got out of the car, stretching our legs for a moment. Vernon was still clutching his ribs when he clambered out. His eyes met mine for a moment.

Reaper cased the place, trying windows on his way toward the back door. Everything was locked. Breaking the glass was too fucking obvious, especially this close to the watchful eyes and ears of the law. Reaper tried a high-hanging window, and he smiled as it slid open.

"Who the hell could fit in there?" Ricky laughed.

Everyone looked at him.

"Oh, come on." Ricky groaned as Reaper put his hands out to give him a leg up. He gripped the windowsill. While hanging from it, he kicked his legs to gain traction and pulled himself through the window. Something clattered and broke when he landed inside, and the gauzy curtains fluttered through the open window as Ricky ran to unlock the door.

"Spidery fuck." Morris laughed as Ricky opened the door, then grabbed him and rubbed his knuckle into the top of his head.

"Yeah, yeah." Ricky batted him away.

When we got inside, we looked around. It looked like an older person lived there . . . if they were even still alive. As long as they weren't lying dead somewhere in the damn house, we didn't care about the grandmotherly decor. But there was no one, not even a body beneath the granny square quilt on the couch.

Reaper tossed me over his shoulder and carried me toward a bedroom. "I don't mean to treat you like you're glass, doll," he said as he laid me down, "but you feel like fuckin' glass."

"I'm not fragile. You know that."

"I know."

"Do you?"

With a groan, I rolled over and looked at the clock on the

wall. It released loud ticks that embedded in my head and raked my damn brain. In reality, it probably wasn't as loud as it sounded to me, but the more upset I got, the louder it seemed to count the seconds.

Shouting broke the tense silence between us.

Reaper looked down the hall. "The fuck is going on?"

He drew his revolver, cocking it as his steps receded. I pulled my pocket pistol from the front of my dress and racked the slide before following after him.

A bullet whizzed by my head and hit the wall as I entered the living room. A hail of gunfire followed it, but I couldn't tell where it was coming from. In a disoriented panic, I slid down the wall and covered my ringing ears. A nauseating pain chased that sound in my head until I nearly vomited.

Morris ran to me and reached for my hand. I pulled my palms from my ears and tried to meet his fingertips, but before I could touch him, he lurched forward and collapsed in a heap.

"Morris!" I screamed.

He turned onto his back, his gray eyes darting.

My eyes searched for a wound beneath his jacket, but I didn't see one. I began to think I'd imagined it. He hadn't been hit. Not Morris. Not *my* Mor—

Blood fanned around him in a shallow pool. Thick crimson that stuck to my shoe as I tried to pull him into me.

"No," I whispered into his ear.

More gunfire erupted, but I couldn't get up. I couldn't stop the tears. Morris turned his head, and a thick rivulet of blood oozed from the corner of his mouth. The gunfire quieted, but the shouting remained. Lawmen yelling their harsh commands through a haze of gun smoke.

Morris choked up more blood, and his eyes kept losing focus as he sputtered. He pulled me close enough that my hair brushed against his lips, painting the strands vermillion. He didn't attempt to stem the flow of life as it left him. We both knew he was a goner. Even so, I wouldn't leave his side as long as he still drew breath. They'd have to rip me away from him.

"Sweets . . ." A cough racked his chest, stifling his words. "My name's Stefforn. I was born . . . and raised in Kansas." He paused and licked his lips, staining his tongue and teeth red. "Thank you for loving me," he whispered, forcing a smile as he closed his eyes and went limp in my arms.

I sobbed, yelling out as I reached for his face. "No! No!"

Hands grabbed at me, and I fought them off, unsure if they belonged to one of my men or the men shooting at us. The men who killed my Morris.

"Fucking bastards!" I screamed, flailing my arms and throwing my body against them.

A hand went around my mouth. "Goddamn it, stop! We have to go." It was Vernon. He dropped his hand.

"But Morris—"

"He's gone, Sil."

Another bullet flew past us, and Vernon returned fire as he dragged me out the back door. A picture caught my eye on the way out. A short, white-haired woman being embraced by a lawman. The new sheriff, full uniform and all. We couldn't have had worse luck when we wound up in the house of the sheriff's mother.

We dove into the car and barreled our way out of town while watching behind us for the sheriff. What other choice did we have?

No one followed.

I looked at the vacant seat in the car, then down at my blood-soaked arms. "His name was Stefforn," I whispered.

Chapter 9

A quarter of my heart was missing. Gone. Taken by the Grim, all because I froze. Morris should have left me in that room. Instead, he left me in a way that was forever imprinted in my mind like a goddamn brand. I felt the heat of the memory against my brain.

I clutched the knife he gave me, running my finger over the intricate grooves in the handle. I set it down on the table beside me. We'd found a house to lay low in, and it sure wasn't no lawman's house this time.

Reaper came into the room and tapped my thigh to encourage me to move over. I scooted toward the arm of the couch, giving Reaper a cushion to sit on. He pulled me into him.

"I'm sorry, doll."

"For what?"

"Everything. Not talking about things I needed to talk about." He shook his head. "Morris." There was a sad longing in his eyes, much like the rest of us had.

Like always, I knew Reaper would want to pour his frustration into me. Even though my heart felt broken, I wanted it. I needed it. Only my men could soothe the ache inside me. I had to surround myself with family and let them love me if I wanted to heal. I knew the risks when I chose this life. I knew that every single day we were together was a gift I shouldn't take for granted. I had come to terms with the risk of losing any of them. I just didn't expect it to be Morris. I thought he'd be able to smooth talk his way out of anything. Maybe even death.

Sometimes I found myself pretending that Morris was on one of his business trips and he'd be back before we knew it. I kept hanging on to that. But he wasn't coming home, and we weren't long for the world ourselves if we continued living the way we were.

I scooped up his knife and held it in a clenched fist. The last thing he'd given me. I would bring it into my battle and use it to obtain vengeance. I'd feel his hand around mine as I did what I had to do to get my revenge. He'd give me the strength I needed.

I wiped away a tear because molls like me couldn't cry. I had to be hard and bury my feelings like them. There was no room for grieving. We'd grieve when things slowed down. If they ever slowed down.

At night, I'd let my tears fall in the solitary moments before Reaper took me to bed. Even as he lay beside me, he put distance between us. He held me differently. He hadn't tried to sleep with me. I didn't know if he couldn't stomach me after what happened with Strawdog's gang or if Morris was just laying too heavy on his mind as well. But I knew it hurt.

I *needed* him. And I needed him to need *me*.

"You don't want anything to do with me," I whispered.

"That's not true, doll. This has nothing to do with you and everything to do with me. I regret leaving you alone that night. Every time I look at you, I see your face, all covered in blood. You had more fear in that moment than when I was about to take you out."

He took the knife from my hand, clutching it for a few moments before laying it on the table. I knew then that it was a little bit of both. It was because of what Strawdog and his gang did to me, but also the empty place in our hearts that Morris had filled.

Reaper drew his pistol from its holster and ran the metal along my discolored cheek. He put it beside the knife, hesitating before withdrawing his fingertips from the gun. He never took that off. He wasn't the type to spill his feelings in the form of words. It was all in his actions. Was he trying to show me his vulnerability?

"I don't make love," Reaper said with a stern voice.

I knew that already, and I wasn't asking him to. He wasn't that type of lover. He was selfish in all the right ways instead. I just needed him to make me forget about the pain. I just needed him to love me.

"But I want to make you feel better," Reaper said as he pushed me down on the couch.

I turned onto my back. "We shouldn't—"

I tried to tell him that we shouldn't fool around, not after everything that happened, but the look in his eyes stopped the words from forming.

I tried again. "What are you—"

He pulled up my dress with rough, scarred hands and buried his face in my pussy. I gasped as his warm breath rolled over my clit. Even if I wanted to, there was no way to pull Reaper away from something he was set on doing, and right then, he was set on putting his mouth on me.

He stopped to look up at me. "I need to show you, really fuckin' show you, that your pussy is as much mine as the day you came here. Schmucks like them could never change that. Would I put my mouth on you if I thought you were dirty?"

He gave me a long lick that made me twitch. I'd never had his tongue on me like that. I never thought I would.

"I love you, doll, even when I ain't showing it."

I knew he did. Reaper wasn't the type of person to fawn all over someone, even if he worshiped the ground they walked on. He showed his adoration the only way he knew how—by letting me past the cold steel walls he'd built around himself or by allowing me to be the one beneath him. When he used his body to shield me from flying bullets or when he killed a man for me . . . that's when I knew he was letting me in. Just because he'd built a fortress around his emotions didn't mean he wasn't worth the effort to rip those damn walls down, because once I got inside, nothing could hurt me.

Reaper dropped his mouth between my legs again, and I gripped the couch as he worked my pussy like I'd never felt. I didn't know if it was because he was so good at it or if it was because it was such a taboo thing for him to do to me, but my nerves were on fire.

His tongue washed away the sadness and the memories of that fateful day. But I knew the moment we stopped and broke away from the pleasure, I'd remember everything all over again. For the moment, the only thing on my mind was Reaper showing me he loved me in a way he never had before.

I gripped his dark hair, pulling him deeper into me. My thighs trembled against his broad shoulders. I tried to keep my moans low between us, but they rose as if they had a mind of their own.

"Fuck," I groaned.

"Don't fight it, doll. If they come, they come," he said before putting his fingers inside me.

I was torn. I didn't mind Vernon or Ricky coming to play, but I didn't want the stern heat of his tongue against my clit to stop. His free hand looped around my thigh and pulled me tighter against his mouth.

As my chest rose off the couch in pleasure, I spotted Vernon in the doorway, smiling with his arms folded across his chest. It was the first hint of a true smile I'd seen since the lawman's mother's house. I leaned up on my elbows so I could keep my eyes on him. My gaze trailed down his body until I landed on the outline of his cock, hard against his zipper. He wiped his chin, eyes equally locked on mine. There was a hint of crazy within them again, and I could only imagine what was playing through his mind. As my back arched and the pleasure nagged at my pelvis, he kept watching me, pushing me toward the edge.

My moans grew and drew Vernon closer until he hovered over me. His hand grazed my cheek before his fingers slid to the button on the front of my dress. He worked it open, allowing the fabric to spread so he could explore beneath it. His touch raced along my nipples as he dropped to his knees and kissed me, his hands rough on my chest. *Oh god.* My body was engulfed in a fire that could burn the whole goddamn house down.

Vernon pulled away from me. "How does that feel? Reaper never puts his mouth on nobody." He squeezed my nipple between his warm fingers, and a whimper of pleasure escaped my throat. "I'll say it for the both of us. I love you, Sil." He released a frustrated groan against my mouth as he kissed me again.

"I love you too," I said through a moan. His words were enough to make me come. Letting the fire consume me, I gripped Vernon's shirt and shuddered against him. "Fuck."

Reaper sat up with a smirk, his chin glistening with my come. He wiped it away with the sleeve of his work shirt before turning me over and pulling me onto my knees.

"What else would make you feel good, doll? Do you want us both?" Reaper asked.

I shook my head. Vernon was too big and rough, even if he

didn't intend to be. "I can't take you both." My eyes met Vernon's as he rose to his feet. "I want Vernon in my mouth."

Reaper unbuttoned his slacks and drew his cock from his boxers. He rubbed against my sensitive pussy, slicking it with my wetness before pushing inside me. I was still twitching.

I pressed my chest against the arm of the couch and looked back at Vernon. He smirked as he stepped toward me, hovering in front of my face. His massive hands worked off the buttons over the tented fabric in the slowest, most sensual way. I drooled with anticipation.

As soon as he touched the tip of his cock to my lips, I froze. I squeezed my eyes closed, trying to calm the sudden acceleration of my heartbeat.

"Reaper, hold up," Vernon said as he squatted in front of me.

Reaper stopped thrusting and laid my hair over my shoulder to look at me.

"Sil, what's the matter?" Vernon's voice was soft and saturated with compassion. He lifted my chin, wiping a tear from my cheek. "Talk to me."

Reaper pulled out of me, the heat of his pelvis still warm against my ass.

My heartbeat was so loud in my ears that I feared it would explode. I didn't realize I was trembling until Reaper sat back and pulled me into him. I sobbed. I let myself cry. Vernon sat beside me on the couch, and I dropped my face into his neck as Reaper's strong arms comforted my body.

"Shh," Vernon whispered, brushing the wet hair from my face. He'd gone limp, and I felt guilt for letting myself break down. "Was it me?" he asked.

I shook my head. "Fucking Strawdog. He rubbed his goddamn dick on my lips."

"I'm going to fucking kill that bastard," Vernon said through clenched teeth.

"No." I flashed my eyes up at him. "He's mine."

A smile crept across Vernon's face at my response.

"May God be with those fuckers," Reaper said with a smirk.

"God doesn't want nothing to do with men like that," I quipped. "The devil sure will welcome them, though."

I shook my weakness off, letting the anger replace the fear and sadness. I needed to focus on pleasure to get past my pain. I leaned over and stroked Vernon, trying to tempt the blood back to his dick. He cocked an eyebrow at me.

"Sil—"

"I'll be fine."

He hardened within my hand, and I bit my lip. Instead of making the move, he let me wrap my lips around him. The panic didn't attack me this time. The position had just been too similar. Too goddamn similar.

He draped his arms over the back of the couch and groaned, dropping his head back. When I popped back onto my knees, Reaper got his invitation too. He had never lost his hard-on, and he pushed himself back into me as if I hadn't stopped him at all. His hands grabbed my hips, and he thrust deep inside me. The salty taste of Vernon in my mouth and the powerful thrusts of Reaper behind me made me forget about everything that had drenched me in fear moments before.

I focused on the pulse of Vernon's hips as he met my mouth and the bounce of my chest against Vernon's thigh as Reaper fucked me. Those men filled the void in my heart with themselves, and I would take all that I could.

"I'm going to beat the hell out of the fucker who touched your fucking mouth," Vernon groaned. "No one touches what's mine."

"Ours," Reaper growled as he hastened his thrusts and chased his pleasure.

Every fiber of my being belonged to them. They coursed through my veins, a life force I could never live without.

Vengeance was coming. Strawdog may have won that one battle, but I was going to win the entire goddamn war.

No mercy.

Chapter 10

We learned the man who couldn't get hard enough to rape me left Strawdog's gang and returned home to his wife and daughter. How ironic. Despite the intense objection from Vernon, I decided I didn't want him killed.

"You sure you wanna leave him breathing?" Vernon asked once more as we passed the state line into New Jersey. "I know *I* want to kill the bastard."

"He didn't do what the others did. He's still a piece of shit, and we're gonna remind him of that, but he doesn't deserve death."

"He participated in an unfair fight, Sil. Had he not—"

"I said no." I turned my head to look out the window once more. I watched the shifting landscape, the trees just starting to change colors. Fall hovered at the edge of the horizon, my favorite time of year.

Vernon grabbed my hand and squeezed. I wanted them to take over this one, and I could only hope they respected my wishes when we reached our destination. I didn't want the fucker killed in front of his goddamn family, even if he deserved it.

The others—the ones who had been inside me—were another story.

When we pulled up to a home on a hill, I leaned out the window to make sure it was the right house. His face was buried beneath the hood of his car as he worked a wrench within the metal labyrinth, but I recognized his body, his stature. Seeing that man allowed the feelings I had pushed down to rise to the surface.

I looked back at Vernon, whose dark eyes gleamed with excitement. He put brass knuckles over his fingers, a sadistic smile on his face. Ricky grabbed a bat from the floorboard and rested it on his lap. Reaper decided his trusty pistol was enough.

We pulled up behind the man's car, and he knocked his head on the open hood as he tried to see who we were. The moment his eyes found mine, his lips tightened. He turned to dart inside, but the cock of Reaper's pistol was enough to make him stop dead in his tracks.

"I wouldn't . . . unless you want to bring this inside to your family," Reaper said.

He turned to face us, his hands moving in a flurry of gestures. "Listen, I'm sorry for what happened to you." He looked at me with a hard gaze. "But I didn't do *that*. That's not who I am."

Reaper took a step toward him. "It's guilt by association. You gang up with schmucks like Strawdog, and you become one of Strawdog's schmucks. Ain't no way to differentiate it. You were a part of what happened to *my* girl, and you put your hands on what's mine."

Ricky stepped forward, spinning the bat at his side. "You have a wife? A daughter?" The man nodded. "Imagine one of them with their skirt hiked up as a line of men take turns raping them."

Vernon made a noise in his throat. "Imagine having to

fucking watch it," he said with such anger in his words. I grabbed his arm to keep him from pushing through and snapping the fool's neck.

The man dropped his gaze, and a blanket of shame covered us. Vernon was ashamed he hadn't protected me. The man was ashamed of participating in something he didn't agree with. I was full of shame because he knew what I looked like, bare and vulnerable.

Ricky broke through the tension with a swing of the bat, landing a well-aimed blow to the man's abdomen. He doubled over with a soundless scream as air scrambled from his lungs. I released Vernon's arm and he charged forward, knocking the man on his back. He leapt on top of him and brought his brass-covered fist against the man's face, over and over, creating a nauseating mix of sounds.

The door to the house opened, and a sweet little girl with bouncy blonde pigtails looked upon the scene with wide, terrified eyes. "Daddy!" she called out, rapping her hands against the screen door.

Vernon looked up, blood dripping from his hand. "Remember that little voice if you ever decide to fuck around with people like Strawdog again. Others wouldn't be so forgiving." Vernon picked him up by his hair, forcing his swollen face to look at me. "Get a good look at her and remember *her* face, because she's the one who let you live."

VERNON RUBBED HIS BLOODY KNUCKLES. When he saw me watching him, he tugged me into him and pressed his lips to mine. "You're so much better than any of us," he said.

"How so?"

"We would have killed that man and left him for his kin to find." Vernon kissed me, his cock hard from the excitement. "We would have murdered him for touching your body, even if he didn't fuck you."

I moaned as his bloody hand raced up my thigh, banishing the moment of hesitation as I watched the crimson-stained skin inch toward my pussy. He leaned me over the back seat. It was a tight squeeze as he crawled between my legs.

"Vernon, leave her alone. You still have the prick's blood on your hands," Reaper commanded.

"She'll tell me if she wants me to stop," Vernon said. He bit into his lower lip. It wasn't like him to ignore our leader, but he was too horny to care about anything but me. "What do you want, Sil?"

"You," I whispered. I felt a pang of guilt over wanting him. Wanting his fingers inside me. As disgusting as it felt, it also seemed like the ultimate "fuck you" to have the blood of an enemy coating the hand that would rip through me with pleasure. "I want your fingers inside me."

Vernon smiled, kissing me as he pushed up my dress and forced his fingers inside me. I groaned as his strong arms worked my body. The violence sent him into a crazed state, and he pushed that insanity into me.

I grabbed his wrist, trying to calm his thrusts, but he pushed my hand away. He fingered me harder, and an intense urge built in my belly with the pressure. He pulled his hand away, making me gush onto the leather seat.

I drew my legs together as I spasmed. "Fuck," I moaned, clutching my throbbing pussy.

Vernon licked my wetness from his fingers, taking in the leftover blood mixed with my come. He rubbed his hand along the dark, wet stain on the front of his slacks and smirked as he kissed me. "I'm not sure what that was, but I loved how it felt around my fingers. I want to feel it around my cock." He unbuttoned his slacks, pulled out his dick, and pushed himself inside me, drilling his hips forward.

When I put my hand on his lower belly to tell him to slow down, he only sped up, pushing deeper and harder as the feeling overwhelmed me once more. He grabbed the base of his cock as I gushed around him, squeezing him and somehow almost pushing him out of me with the force of my orgasm. He drew his hips back, letting me flood the head of his cock. Another thrust drove me into the seat as he buried himself inside me once more.

He wrapped his arm around me, forcing me to keep every inch of him inside me. "Goddamn it, Sil," he groaned as he let himself come, my pussy pleading for every drop.

We were sick fucks. And we had only just begun.

Chapter 11

"I wish you'd stay back for this one, love," Ricky said as he wrapped me in his arms. I met his gaze and lost myself in his blue eyes. There wasn't a chance in hell I'd stay behind. I was one of them, and they were a part of me. I wouldn't let pieces of myself walk out that goddamn door without me, especially when everything was going down because of *me*.

"I know you want your revenge, but if something happens to you—" Ricky tightened his lips, cutting off his own sentence. "I can't lose you."

"If death comes for us, we go together."

I adjusted the pistol on my thigh before reaching out and catching a Thompson that Vernon tossed my way. I checked if it was loaded before letting it hang by my side.

My boys smirked at me. Nothing was more dangerous than an angry woman with a goddamn automatic and a thirst for blood.

I grabbed Morris' knife from the table and tucked it into the twist of my braid for good luck. He'd be right by my side during what we were about to do if he could. I wished that hell had visiting hours so he could bolster me with his confidence.

Ricky racked his sawed-off shotgun, Reaper made sure his pistol was loaded, and Vernon wielded the powerful BAR as we prepared to leave. Strawdog and his gang were doing a hand-off with another small group in the warehouse off the speakeasy, and we planned to make a little visit. That meant there was another group to deal with—people who weren't meant to be in the fray—and that was a problem. Ricky had an idea to spare those men, but I worried it would only get our hands bloodier.

We got in the car and drove toward the speakeasy. I rubbed my sweaty palms along my dress. Ricky pulled me into him and kissed my forehead. Just as Ricky opened his mouth to speak, I put a finger over his lips. "We aren't turning back," I told him.

The vengeance. The retribution. I needed it. It was the only way I could put those nightmares to rest.

We pulled onto the dark road in front of the speakeasy. Men in suits meandered about, smoking cigarettes. Legality meant nothing when it came to Prohibition. If you wanted something bad enough, you'd find a way. You always found a way.

Ricky turned his head, snapping his gaze to a well-dressed man who demanded attention. "That's him. The leader of the leggers coming tonight."

"He doesn't look too friendly, angel," I said as I peered over his shoulder.

Before I could grab the sleeve of his jacket and hold him back, he was already out of the car. He closed the door, shielded his face from the rain, and jogged across the street toward the man. When he reached the brick wall, he leaned against it and started talking.

The older man—hardened from being in the business

long before alcohol became illegal—stared at Ricky as he gestured toward the car and explained our situation. There was no expression on his face. The man passed Ricky a cigarette, and even though I'd never seen him smoke, he took it and accepted the matches. He covered them with his hand as he struck the match and lit the cigarette, exhaling smoke as he dropped his head against the wall. The man laughed beside him.

Come on, Ricky. I watched my sweet angel puff on the cigarette, trying to buy passage for a clean kill. We didn't want a war with no one else.

The man put his hand out to Ricky, and once he squelched the cigarette, Ricky shook it. I took a deep breath. A laugh and a handshake didn't guarantee a thing, and trusting a stranger's word was never wise in any business, let alone this one.

Ricky ran back to the car, pushing me over as he got in. "We're good. They're going to do the trade off and skedaddle. They don't want no trouble."

"What'd you tell him?" I asked.

"That we got business with Strawdog for what he did to you. Once he found out what they did, there was just an understanding. You don't fuck with another man's woman. Especially not like that. They agreed to leave the door unlocked on their way out."

Vernon made a noise that sounded like he didn't hold much belief in our plan. He was mistrustful of most people, so that was no surprise. Reaper wasn't entirely convinced either. Ricky was the only one filled with hope, and I wished he'd realize how fucking shitty people were before it was too late.

People poured from the speakeasy's side entrance as the night dredged on. They were stumbling drunk by the time they pulled themselves away from the music and obscurity behind the metal door and brick walls. My heart hammered in my chest as we watched the other gang bring their goods into the warehouse in the side building. Crates of liquor. Liquid gold. It felt like hours before they finally left with pockets full of cash.

We got out of the car and walked across the street, keeping our guns concealed against our sides. The men tucked them haphazardly beneath their jackets. I kept mine on my side in the shadows.

"Ready?" Reaper asked as he gripped the metal door. He pushed the door open after we gave him a nod, and we made our way down the dark hallway. Drops of water fell from the overhead pipes, masking our steps. The scent of mildew and decayed wood saturated the air.

We turned the corner into the warehouse and were met with a sea of metal. Strawdog and his gang had their guns drawn on us. There were more men than we expected—men we'd never met and had no fight with—but when they drew and racked, they brought the fight to them.

Fuck.

"This is why you don't trust people, Ricky," Reaper hissed as he drew his pistol and shot a man in the head who had the nerve to cock his gun in our direction.

Vernon and Reaper sprayed bullets, and I raised my Thompson and shot a man that came from the shadows beside me. The stock hopped against my shoulder. The sounds ricocheted off the metal walls, creating an overwhelming sound that triggered memories I didn't want to remember.

The explosion of gunshots rang around us, whizzing by. Vernon sent a hail of bullets across the warehouse, making men scatter for cover. When his magazine was empty, he grabbed one from his jacket pocket and loaded his next rounds. We hid behind crates riddled with bullet holes. Liquid spilled from them until the swirling, mixed smell of alcohol and gunpowder made me drunk. I leaned out of my cover as footsteps crept closer, and sent bullets into a man until he dropped. Casings pinged against the floor and skittered across the concrete.

"You are so fuckin' sexy, doll," Reaper said with a smirk.

"Show me later," I said, my drum nearly empty. Vernon tossed a stick mag my way, and I reloaded the Thompson.

From somewhere beyond the crates, Strawdog's voice called out in pain. No. He couldn't die like that. That would be too easy for him. We left our hiding spot and went toward the cries.

I found Whiskey hiding beneath a crate, his hands trembling as he lifted them. Vernon found Strawdog, bleeding from the arm. He shot the crate beside Strawdog's head, and a fountain of moonshine sped from the hole. It splashed onto his wound, making him scream out.

"The irony," Vernon snarled.

"Where's the third piece of shit?" Reaper asked.

"Dead," Strawdog said.

I grabbed the gun from Whiskey and tossed it aside. "That's a shame."

Ricky grabbed Whiskey by the jacket and dragged him over to Strawdog, tossing him beside his boss. Blood-tinged alcohol spread around our feet. He kept his gun trained on Whiskey while we focused on Strawdog.

"Pick him up," I said to Reaper and Vernon as I motioned toward Strawdog with my gun.

They lifted him by his arms. Strawdog kept his jaw set, unwilling to plead for his life as I walked toward him and dropped to my knees. Bloody liquor soaked through my skirt, but I didn't care. Retribution was worth more than the dress. I flashed my eyes up at him as I set the Thompson aside and unbuckled his belt.

"Do you remember what I told you?" I asked, biting my lip. I undid the button on his slacks.

"You're just a whore," Strawdog hissed.

Vernon sank his thumb into the bullet wound in Strawdog's arm, digging around until the coward cried out. It was music to my ears.

"You really don't remember?" I asked as I pulled his cock from his boxers. He was limp—too filled with fear for blood to reach his dick. I wrapped a hand around him.

With pulsing cheeks, Vernon's jaw clenched, but he didn't interfere.

I searched through my hair until I grasped Morris' knife, and I let my fingers play over the grooves in the blade. Thoughts of Morris steadied my hand. His strength fueled me. All of theirs did, but especially his. He died trying to save me, and this man would die while *I* saved the parts of me he shattered when he forced himself between my legs. A sadistic swirl of excitement blossomed in my gut.

I brandished the knife, flipped it, and sliced through Strawdog's dick before he knew what was happening or could react. Blood spurted onto me, spraying my chest with warm crimson.

"I told you I'd rip your dick off, you piece of shit," I snarled at him, flicking his blood off my hands.

Strawdog's scream broke through the silence, louder than any gunshot I'd ever heard.

"Oh fuck," Vernon said, his eyes wide. His cock was as hard as could be.

They dropped Strawdog and let him slide down the crates and land in the liquor and blood beneath his feet.

"Oh god, oh fucking god!" Strawdog screamed, clutching his hands to his crotch. Blood seeped around his fingers.

I turned to Whiskey, whose eyes were wide and terrified as I rubbed the tip of Strawdog's dick in my hand, painting my palm with more blood. I put my knife to his throat, and he pissed his goddamn pants. The yellow liquid saturated his slacks and mixed with the rest of the fluids on the ground.

"Open your mouth," I said to him. Whiskey shook his head, cutting into his own neck. Blood dripped in a line down his throat. "Open your goddamn mouth!" I pushed further into his skin.

He finally spread his lips enough for me to shove the head of Strawdog's severed dick into his fucking mouth. Blood snaked down his chin.

"Chew it."

Whiskey did as I commanded, his retching breaking the silence around us. Strawdog's screams had stopped once he'd fallen unconscious.

Vernon wrapped his hand around mine and eased the knife away from Whiskey's throat, pocketing it before tossing the BAR to Reaper. He raised my skirt, and while keeping his eyes locked on Whiskey's defeated face, he bent me over one of the crates, his hand racing to free his cock so he could fuck me. He made Whiskey watch as he slid his hand down the front of my neck, leaving a trail of blood behind. He pushed inside me.

"You thought you could break her? Not my moll. Not our girl. You only gave her the flame she needed to light you all on fire." Vernon groaned into my ear as he slammed his hips into me. "She's a crazy son of a bitch, like the rest of us. Dropping to her knees when facing the prick who raped her. Disarming what he used as a weapon. Making you feel the shame she felt."

I moaned at the truths he spilled from his clenched jaw. I was fucked up, but so were they, and that was why we worked.

He reached his arm around my waist and palmed me. "You wanna see how a real man can make her come? A fucking *wop*, as you so lovingly called me?"

"You're hardly Italian," I said with a moan as his blood-coated hand stroked me. I looked back at him as his thrusts grew hungrier. We were both getting close.

"Come for us, Sil. For him too," Vernon growled, raising his chin toward Whiskey. "Especially for him."

I came hard, with more eyes on me than I'd ever had before. I expected Vernon to follow my pleasure, but he pulled out and finished himself in his hand. With a crazy look in his eyes, he smirked at me before his face twisted in anger. He walked to Whiskey and slapped his cheek, smearing his face with the degradation he deserved.

Vernon motioned toward Ricky, who handed him the shotgun. Vernon took great pleasure in blowing Whiskey's brains out. His expression washed with a look I only saw after I made him come. Blood splattered everywhere, and wood splintered behind him. He leaned over the body and spit down at what was left of the man's face.

Vernon handed the shotgun back to Ricky and wiped his hands on his pants. Blood and whatever was left of his come trailed across the fabric.

"What about him?" I asked as I looked at Strawdog, whose breathing was slow and shallow.

"He'll either bleed out or spend the rest of his life dickless," Ricky said as he tugged at my arm. "Which is honestly worse than dying."

I agreed. I would accept that vengeance. He'd either die or wish he was dead for the rest of his life. And he could never rape another woman.

"Let's get the fuck out of here," Reaper said as he shook his head. "Crazy bastards. That includes you, doll."

We turned and started toward the door, but the third man

—the one we thought was dead, the last one who forced his way inside me—stepped in front of us with a pistol drawn. He aimed for Ricky, and I leapt in front of him. I had to protect my angel. The bullet sank into my shoulder in front of Ricky's chest. It took a moment for the pain to catch up to the sound of the shot and the glare from the muzzle.

"You fucking piece of shit!" Ricky screamed as he racked the shotgun and stepped beyond me, leaving himself vulnerable as he fired his gun without a moment of hesitation. The other man curled his finger around the trigger and sent a bullet into Ricky's abdomen.

I was so damn proud of Ricky for protecting me, but fuck, it hurt to see.

They crumpled to the ground, the other man already dead. I screamed as I dropped to Ricky's side, ignoring every ounce of pain in my body so I could comfort his. He clutched his abdomen, blood seeping around his fingers. His lip trembled as he looked up at me. He smiled and reached a hand toward my arm to hold pressure against my wound.

"No, angel. No. Don't worry about me." I turned toward the boys. "I can't do this again. I can't."

Ricky's face was paper white. His chest heaved as more blood rose from the depths of him. "I love you, Silvia. More than the breath in my body." He choked out the words.

I couldn't do this again. I refused.

Chapter 12

I had little hope for Ricky. By the time we scooped him up and Reaper dropped us off at the house, he was in rough shape. I didn't know how someone his size could lose so much goddamn blood and still look at me with the softest eyes. His lids kept closing, and I kept pushing him to stay awake. I didn't want to stay at the house, but Reaper had to get him to a hospital outside of the city without drawing more attention to us. Vernon stayed back with me.

I sat on the couch, still covered in the blood of too many goddamn people as Vernon wrapped my arm. I couldn't take not knowing if he was alive or not. I was drowning in grief and guilt, and I'd have given anything to have held him back and let one of the others make the shot. I'd never seen that kind of anger cross sweet Ricky's face. It was as if another person had taken hold of him.

"What were you thinking, Sil?" Vernon asked.

"That's just it, I wasn't thinking," I said in a very Vernon-esque way. "I just had to protect him."

"If it were you—"

I snapped my gaze up to him. "What do you mean by that? Do you think Ricky's dead?"

"Sil . . ." Vernon swallowed the lump in his throat.

"Don't Sil me, Vernon. Tell me the truth."

Neither of us knew for sure, and we wouldn't know until one or both of them came home, but the look on Vernon's face told me too many things I didn't want to hear. *No. Not my angel.* Ricky was too fucking good for us. Too goddamn special.

My heart was silent. I couldn't even hear or feel the beats in my chest.

"It just didn't look good, is all."

"How can you be so cavalier about it? He's our family!"

Vernon grabbed my chin and lifted it. "What do you want from me, Sil? We did this for you, and you knew the risk we were taking. We all did. He went out trying to protect you. That would have meant the world to him."

"How can I live with that?" I said with a defeated drop in my shoulders.

"We have to, because that's what we do. That's who we are. Death is a part of this life."

"Ricky shouldn't be in this life!" I fought back tears.

"He belongs as much as you and I. Ricky wasn't the soft, meek man you thought he was. Ricky's brother was one of the toughest sons a bitches I've ever met. That was always in him, coursing through his veins. He was one of us."

Vernon finished bandaging my arm and pulled me into him. "You are incredible, Sil. Any one of us would have died protecting you. We'd *all* die to protect you."

Tires rolled over the driveway, and I held my breath. Vernon pulled me into him, preparing me for the news I didn't want to hear. News he knew I couldn't handle. Not so soon after losing my Morris.

"Sil, look at me," he said as he grabbed my face, turning me away from the door. "If Ricky is gone—"

"Don't. Don't even say it, Vernon." I pushed his hand away.

Reaper came in, his dress shirt stained with blood. He looked weathered and exhausted, as if he hadn't slept at all. My heart sank in my chest when I saw his tightly drawn lips.

Not my angel. No.

Tears fell freely down my cheeks and splattered on my chest, and I did nothing to stop them. Vernon made a move to pull me into him, but I pushed him away. Steps came from behind Reaper, and I got a glimpse of Ricky. My angel.

I leapt off the couch and pushed Reaper aside, needing to see him with my own eyes to believe he wasn't a ghost. Stained bandages wound around his bare abdomen, and his jacket was slung over his shoulder. He shuffled from pain as he walked, but it was him, in the flesh.

I wrapped my arms around him, ignoring the pain in my arm. He flinched against my touch but hugged me tighter despite it.

"Oh, angel." I sobbed into his chest. "I thought—"

"It'd take a lot more than a .32 to keep me from you, love," he said with a pained laugh.

I kissed his mouth, reveling in the feeling of him in my arms again. I turned to Reaper and hugged him. "Thank you," I whispered.

"Don't thank me, doll. We'd do anything for you." He kissed my forehead.

I looked back at Vernon. He smiled and pulled Ricky into him.

"I'm still broken, you know," Ricky said through clenched teeth. Instead of releasing him, Vernon hugged him for an extra moment before ruffling his hair as he pushed him away.

There was so much love in that room that I thought my heart might explode from my chest. We were so crazy, so reckless, so goddamn in love. They were my family, and they never had to wonder if I'd walk through fire with them. We journeyed through the flames of hell and dined with the devil, and that was the life we chose. Yes, even my angel.

Four syllables. We were retribution.

Epilogue

I have no idea how we did it. The rest of us kept alive to see Prohibition repealed. I got married on the fifth of December, the day the law passed. We actually got married on the eighth, but a little convincing marked our official day as the fifth.

Who did I marry?

Ricky, of course. The only one who didn't have his face posted all over the city. He hung our marriage certificate in the living room of the home we bought. Quaint and unsuspecting, which was exactly how we wanted it.

I placed Morris' knife on top of the bulky frame. I later found out more about Morris... well, Stefforn. He was one of the FBI's most wanted. He'd done a bit of everything. I struggled to accept that the man I gave my body to so many times was the same man so capable of violence. Stefforn had once been a monster, but when he was Morris, that beast loved me. He was still such a part of my very essence, and I knew he was sitting at hell's gate, flipping a coin and waiting for us.

Vernon came up behind me and scooped me up, kissing me on the mouth. I pushed his hands away. "I'm a classy married woman now," I told him, my chin raised. "I respect the sanctity of marriage."

"The hell you do, my little heathen. A classy married woman wouldn't have made me come on her honeymoon," he said with a raise of an eyebrow.

"Or me," Reaper said as he walked in, leaning against the doorframe.

It was the best of both worlds. Ricky and I had a beautiful front we were able to hide behind. We looked like a normal married couple, and Vernon and Reaper were his "brothers" who lived with us. If anyone knew I fucked all of them—that I loved each one of them—we'd be broken apart. Forced away because of social mores.

I could never be with one man.

Vernon was my perfect kind of crazy. Reaper was the safety I'd always needed. And my angel? Ricky was an embodiment of all that was right with the world.

A knock on the door startled us. We needed to get used to that if we had any hopes of being normal. Normal people had visitors. Reaper kept his hand on the butt of his pistol as he went to the door. I reminded myself to breathe as it creaked open, letting the sunlight creep across the floor.

Reaper was silent, and his posture changed as if he was seeing a ghost.

When I heard the voice, I knew he was seeing exactly that. Morris. Some fucking how, some fucking way, he stood on the doorstep. It seemed impossible. A cruel joke. Punishment for all the shit I'd done.

I didn't believe it until Morris pushed past Reaper, ran to me, and picked me up in a relentless hug. He spun me around before kissing me. Only once I felt his mouth, familiar and alive, did I know he was real.

I looked around at the others. Their expressions radiated with just as much confusion as I felt. Reaper's brow wrinkled.

Vernon stopped smiling, too stunned to respond. Ricky looked absolutely dumbstruck. He brushed a hand through his hair and exhaled, trying to breathe away his disbelief.

"But . . . how?" I choked out through the warm heat of tears behind my eyes. "I saw you . . . I saw you—"

"Oh, sweets, not even the devil could keep me from you." He leaned back and brushed the hair from my face. "The lawman showed some mercy that day and got me to the hospital. By the grace of God, I'm here today."

"You're on the most wanted list. How did you escape?"

"No, Stefforn is on the most wanted list. Morris is not. I was still in hot shit from the shootout, though. Talked up a nurse, all sweet and such, and she was willing to look the other way while I walked outta there."

I was in what felt like a permanent state of shock. All the tears I cried over him. All the memories of his death that followed my every step like an overbearing shadow. And somehow, here he was. As if nothing had happened.

"If that's true, why haven't you shown up before now?" I dropped my gaze.

"Sweets, I had to lay low for a bit. I was worried I'd never see you guys again, but then I saw the announcement of your marriage. Though, I would have been the one to make you my wife . . . if I wasn't such a criminal. That's the reason I never told any of you my name. I never wanted you guys to find out who I really was, but especially not you, sweets."

He spotted his knife on top of the framed marriage license. He picked it up and put it in his pocket, where it belonged. "That man, the one who killed all those people, that's not me. That hadn't been me in a long time. But I didn't want you guys to think I was capable of that anymore. But you, sweets? I didn't want you to have a hint of fear from my touch. If I knew the lawmen would end up being my goddamn heroes"— his face twisted in disgust—"I would have never told you.

Stefforn would have gone with me to hell where we both belonged."

I stood there, dizzy with every emotion, my mouth stuck open as I processed it all.

How could I recover from a loss that devastated me to my very core? How could I undo all this guilt when it was all for nothing in the best possible way? I felt insane. All that time washed away. The pain of grief. Walking around with a heart that refused to beat, only to have what would force it back into rhythm standing in front of me.

"Morris, I don't know how to . . . how to accept this," I stammered.

"Just tell me you're still mine," he said as he flashed his soul-searching gray eyes at me.

They ripped apart my hesitation. Instead of responding with words, I tugged him into me until I could hear the thump of his chest against my ear. Of course I was still his. I had never stopped being his. Even when he was gone, I knew he was waiting for me, and that I would be waiting for him.

My heart echoed in my ears, beating in ways it hadn't since I saw him take what I thought was his last breath. It's as if having all four of them there with me made up each chamber of my heart.

Only with all four of them could I be whole.

Connect with Lauren

Check out LaurenBiel.com to sign up for the newsletter and get VIP (free and first) access to Lauren's spicy novellas and other bonus content!

Join the group on Facebook to connect with other fans and to discuss the books with the author. Visit http://www.facebook.com/groups/laurenbieltraumances for more!

Lauren is now on Patreon! Get access to even more content and sneak peeks at upcoming novels. Check it out at www.patreon.com/LaurenBielAuthor to learn more!

Acknowledgments

A thank you to my husband, who continues to support my journey to the dark side.

A special shout out to my editor who continues to help me make my stories come to life.

Thank you to my readers for giving me requests for stories and continually challenging me and helping me grow! Love you all!

A Message from Lauren

My next novel is going to be something a little different. You guys are used to traveling down the darker roads with me, but I think it's time to take a slight detour. Think of it as a pit stop on this journey. Instead of a giant ball of yarn or the world's largest rocking chair, I plan to share one of my early manuscripts with you.

AfterWife is a dramedy that follows Everett Enders after the untimely death of his wife, Renee. Only...she's not quite ready to pass on just yet. Renee has a secret, and until she makes amends, she's stuck haunting her husband. Dating, jerking off, visiting a strip club and trying to get laid—all of these things must be done with his ghostly wife in tow.

We'll get back to the darker roads soon, but if I didn't put this novel out, my husband wouldn't let me hear the end of it. Make sure you join my Facebook group to see the memes he's been bombarding me with for months. They're a laugh riot, just like *AfterWife* (according to my editor).

Also by Lauren Biel

To view Lauren Biel's complete list of books, visit: https://www.amazon.com/Lauren-Biel/e/B09CQYDK87

About the Author

Lauren Biel is an author with several titles in the works. When she's not working, she's writing. When she's not writing, she's spending time with her husband, her friends, or her pets. You might also find her on a horseback trail ride or sitting beside a waterfall in Upstate New York. When reading her work, expect the unexpected.

To be the first to know about her upcoming titles, please visit www.LaurenBiel.com.

Made in the USA
Middletown, DE
28 June 2023